SUSPICION ON THE STRIP
A JJ KAMARAS COZY MYSTERY

JOY PATRICK

MERMAID SISTERS PUBLISHING, INC.

Copyright © 2024 by Joy Patrick
All rights reserved.
No part of this book may be reproduced in any form or by any electronic or mechanical means, including information storage and retrieval systems, without written permission from the author, except for the use of brief quotations in a book review.

* * *

WRITTEN IN COLLABORATION
WITH
J. CROSTHWAITE

* * *

CHAPTER 1

*I*n the blink of an eye, how life had changed.

JJ stared out the window of Rebecca's garage, contemplating the new challenge that was upon her.

"You ready?"

JJ brushed a lock of hair aside and stared up at the wide, glossy camera lens.

"Smile," Rita called out, gesturing with her hands.

JJ lowered her chin and gave a wide smile.

Rita grinned. "Perfect. Just like that."

JJ managed another vague approximation of a smile. She had never been a huge fan of photographs. Even in her time as a professional gymnast, she'd shied away from attention and the camera as much as she could manage. But since meeting Rita Natale, a bonafide expert in the digital marketing world, and watching her work her magic to catapult the tiny Kamaras Grill onto the map during her fundraiser for the gymnastics championship a few months earlier, JJ was keeping an open mind. Actually, the entire Natale family had had quite an impact on her—including Aunt Constanza Natale, a long-time, high-ranking police investigator in Florence, Italy, and especially Rita's cousin and JJ's first encounter with their clan, the dashing Tony Natale.

JJ blinked as the eye of the camera flashed brightly.

"That's a good one." Rita's grin broadened.

"Can I see?" she asked.

Rita gave an enthusiastic nod, beckoning her forward. "Of course."

JJ stared down at the large digital camera screen at a woman who looked like a more sassy, more glamorous version of the one she saw in the mirror. She raised an eyebrow. "That *is* good."

Rita smiled. "I told you. By the time we're done here, you'll have the best profile pictures in the business."

JJ returned to the wooden stool that was propped in the center of the living room. It had been three months since she'd returned from Italy, where the Natale family had hosted JJ, Rebecca, and Gwen Q. Though Rita was a godsend for the media and branding end of their venture, it was Aunt Constanza who had truly encouraged it.

Kamaras, Brannigan & Quinones—her own detective agency.

Rita's camera flashed several more times in rapid succession before she glanced down with a satisfied look at the photos. "Okay JJ, I think that's a wrap. Next up!"

With Gwen Q and JJ's photos completed, Rebecca stepped up next, her hunter green pantsuit highlighting her auburn tresses. "My turn?"

Rita nodded. "Your turn."

Today Rebecca's garage, aka the Batcave, was decorated with burgundy panels and soft mood lights, while the trio had incorporated classic detective accoutrements into their sleek outfits. JJ held an oversized antique magnifying glass in front of a perfectly tailored, midnight blue suit dress, Rebecca topped off her pantsuit with a short, tweed cape, and Gwen Q somehow made a Deerstalker hat look like it belonged on the cover of Vogue. All told, it was a style Rebecca termed *Sherlockian chic*.

The entire exercise began when they asked Rita Natale for her opinion on their website. One look was all it took before Rita insisted that a total makeover was essential. Short informational videos, social media handles—Rita had it all mapped out. In just three weeks, they had seen their followers on Facebook and Instagram skyrocket and had received more calls in the last four days than they had in the two months prior. Make no mistake, Rita Natale was good. She took a deep and personal interest in JJ's success on account of three things—first, because JJ was a close friend of her cousin Tony; second, because JJ had saved her uncle from choking while dining at the Kamaras Grill; and third, because JJ solved the murder of her cousin Vito at an opera performance in Italy. Whenever JJ offered to pay, Rita had the same rebuff. "I owe you more than you owe me, Julia."

Rita didn't seem to realize that Tony and JJ had become more than just acquaintances. How much more, or exactly how to define their status, remained unclear. JJ had been down this road before. Her last attempt to keep things easy-breezy ended up with her then-love interest, Max, falling for her beautiful rival, Priti Patel. Even though the relationship was long since over and Max had taken a job out west, she'd wondered, looking back, if it would have turned out differently if she had been more assertive with her desire to be exclusive. With Tony, it seemed to be playing out all over again. They went out regularly, always had a fabulous time, and the attraction seemed very mutual. However, there was little talk of how they spent their off time, or with whom. So, JJ assumed that their official status remained *casual*.

Rita splashed the final photo spread of the new detective partners onto a large screen. Predictably, Gwen Q looked the best in the final edit of the pictures. With seemingly no effort or forethought at all, just her own eclectic style and magnetism, her pictures looked like something right off the red carpet.

The three women stood shoulder-to-shoulder as they glanced at the finished shots on the screen.

"I still can't believe we're really doing this," JJ said.

Gwen Q's eyes widened. "Neither can I."

Rebecca grinned. "I knew it would happen. Under the wise direction of our beloved Sherlock here," she said pointing at JJ, "we're three for three cracking murder cases. About time we joined the big leagues."

A phone rang on the table behind them.

JJ glanced over her shoulder at the cell phone as it vibrated across the table. "A client?"

Rebecca rubbed her hands together. "Let's hope so."

JJ put the phone on speakerphone. "Hello, Kamaras, Brannigan, and Quinones. How can I help you?"

"Greetings, my dear, brilliant detective."

JJ grinned. "Constanza!"

Constanza laughed. "Ciao!"

Rita drew in close. "Is that Aunt Constanza?"

JJ nodded and they all huddled around to speak to the Italian woman who'd become their friend, mentor, and biggest supporter.

"How is the detective business?" Constanza asked.

"Well . . ." JJ began with a frown. "Could be better."

The truth was that business was going pretty well so far. They had three clients already, which was more than they could have reasonably hoped to expect in their first three months of operation. Before JJ had solved the murder in Italy, she'd have placed herself somewhere in the D grade of celebrity for her detective pursuits, but since returning from Europe, she felt firmly in the C category. A feature on both local and international news had thrust her firmly into Jim Thorpe's consciousness and beyond, making her even more famous than when she won the Pan Am Games in gymnastics over ten years back.

All sorts of calls flooded in when they first opened the detective agency, mostly from true crime enthusiasts who were dying to share their deepest conspiracy theories. Still, they did manage to get three legitimate clients. The first was Roger Aaronson, a man in his sixties who had called to report the theft of three valuable baseball cards from his prized collection. The second was from a successful realtor, Brenda Jace, who suspected that her husband Chad—also a realtor— was having an affair. The third was Caitlyn Banes, a young town councilwoman who suspected foul play in the Jim Thorpe Office of Planning and Development with the controversial approval of a slew of low-rises along the edge of east Jim Thorpe.

So overall, the new agency was off to a solid start, but JJ felt as though there was much more they could be doing.

"We have three cases, so I suppose you could say business is going pretty well," JJ said to Constanza.

Something in her tone must have given her away because Constanza cleared her throat mockingly. "Not quite as exciting as a murder investigation though, is it?"

JJ hesitated a moment. "I suppose not."

"That's the truth of this business. The big cases don't come around every day, but when they do, you have to be ready. Make sure your mind stays sharp. When the big investigation comes your way, don't be caught sleeping."

"Right." JJ gave a deep nod. "I won't." She couldn't help but smile at the thought of it. "So, how's *your* business since coming out of retirement?"

"A new lease on life, I'd say. I'm busier than I ever thought possible . . . and couldn't be happier." Constanza hesitated for a moment. "But never *too* busy. Remember, I'm always here if you need me."

"I do remember. You're my Inspector Lestrade, after all."

Constanza chuckled, and though JJ couldn't see her, she knew there was a glint of satisfaction on her face at the reference to being Sherlock Holmes's older mentor. "Well, I just wanted to check in on you. Keep your head up. The big fish will come swimming."

"Thanks for the vote of confidence," JJ said. "I think we needed that."

They ended the call with Constanza and decided to indulge in a semi-celebratory lunch at the Kamaras Grill, inviting Rita to join them.

When they walked into the restaurant, JJ's mother Athena stood behind the reception desk and smiled at each of them in turn. "Well, look at you girls. You all look beautiful."

JJ offered a sheepish thanks. Her mother loved it when she wore make-up and glammed up her usual look.

They headed to their customary corner booth and Jamal, the head waiter and occasionally sous chef at the restaurant, gave them a welcoming smile. "I'll be back to take your orders in a minute, but let me bring some hummus out first."

"Excellent." JJ smiled. "Thanks, Jamal."

Hummus was always a standing order, no matter what the occasion. JJ and her father had worked together to make the perfect blend of old and new flavors in their house-style hummus.

Athena approached their table holding a small black box. "I have something for the lovely detectives." She slid the box across the table.

JJ pulled the lid open to reveal three stacks of white business cards with their names written in black and gold script. JJ pulled a card out and studied its thick, matte finish.

"They're perfect," JJ breathed. "Thank you, Mom."

Athena smiled wide. "I'm glad you like them."

Just then, JJ's phone rang and she glanced down at it. The call was from realtor Brenda Jace. JJ leaned back from the table and answered.

"Hello?"

Brenda's voice was thick with worry on the phone. "Chad just left the house. He says he's going for a meeting but I know it's to see *her*." The last word was hissed with more than a little dose of malice.

JJ drew in a breath. "How long ago did he leave?"

Brenda's breath quickened audibly. "About five minutes ago."

JJ glanced down at her watch. The Jaces lived ten minutes away, so if Chad took Vermont Street in his Tesla, she could catch him passing the Grill and tail him to his supposed mistress. She pulled out Chad's business card with his picture on it that Brenda had given her.

"I just need proof," Brenda urged. "If I have proof, I can leave him. I'm sick of this."

JJ sighed and rose to her feet. "I'm on it, Mrs. Jace." She dropped the call and turned to Rebecca. "Could I borrow your car?"

Rebecca raised an eyebrow. "What for?"

"Brenda Jace's husband. I think he might be passing by here en route to his mistress—I want to get some proof."

"So you want to tail him?"

JJ gave a small, single-shouldered shrug. "Yes."

"Oh, I am *definitely* coming," Rebecca said.

The two glanced at Gwen Q and Rita, who both offered polite refusal.

"My mind is set on that hummus," Rita said.

Gwen Q nodded. "Mine, too."

JJ cringed as she watched Jamal emerge from the kitchen with a fresh bowl of hummus.

"We'll be right back," JJ said. "Save some hummus for us."

Gwen Q raised her hands in surrender.

JJ laughed and shook her head. She left with Rebecca, her mother giving them both a confused glance as they strode toward the door.

JJ mouthed the word *work* as they passed by so as not to interrupt her conversation with a newly arrived family, but couldn't be sure she had seen it.

"I'll drive," Rebecca said with a smile as they stepped outside.

She had started an advanced driving course six weeks ago, and JJ just knew she was itching for an opportunity to show them all her new skills.

Rebecca's Dodge Durango was parked at the edge of the street. They hopped inside and she turned the engine on.

JJ pointed toward the adjoining street. "If I recall correctly, he drives a Tesla. If we're lucky, he'll drive right by us and get stopped at the traffic light just ahead. From there, we follow him and see if he really does have a mistress."

Rebecca nodded and smiled mischievously. "Let's hope we get lucky then."

As though on perfect cue, a dark Tesla rolled slowly by and JJ's eyes widened. "That's him."

Rebecca lowered her chin as she peeled out down the street. The Tesla had just whizzed through a green light. Rebecca hesitated.

"What are we waiting for?" JJ urged.

Rebecca glanced at her. "I'm not going until you say it."

"Say what?" JJ asked.

Rebecca didn't look at her. "You know."

JJ pointed through the windscreen urgently. "We're losing him."

Rebecca gripped the steering wheel. "You have to say it, JJ."

The car had almost totally disappeared from view. JJ's shoulders drooped as she let out a resigned sigh. "Follow that car."

Rebecca still didn't move. "And…?"

JJ shook her head and couldn't help a faint smile. "And step on it!"

Rebecca laughed and floored it after the Tesla.

CHAPTER 2

They rounded a tight corner at frightening speed and Rebecca gave an almost feral grin. JJ gripped the handle above the car window as though it was life itself.

"What sort of driving lessons have you been taking?" JJ shrieked.

Rebecca lowered her chin and leaned forward. "I've been doing a little extra credit homework."

The engine roared as they tore down the road and, finally, the Tesla appeared in the distance.

"There he is," JJ said, pointing. She took a second look and her heart sank. It wasn't Chad Jace at all. The man in the driver's seat was at least fifty pounds heavier than Chad and had hair dyed a deep orange-red. "That isn't him."

Rebecca smoothly decreased her speed. "What?"

"It isn't him," JJ said, a note of utter defeat in her voice. "Wrong car."

Rebecca slowed to a crawl. "Oh."

Just then, a dark green Toyota idled past. The sound of Ricky Martin's *Livin' La Vida Loca* blared from its fully open windows. JJ's eyes widened as she caught a look at the driver.

"That's him," she said. "That's definitely him."

"I thought you said Tesla." Rebecca's expression was serious as she caught up to the car, then expertly lowered her speed to keep a careful distance between the two vehicles.

JJ stole a breath and finally let go of the grab handle. "Remind me never to let you drive again."

Rebecca smiled triumphantly. "I feel so alive."

The Toyota pulled off the freeway, down an uninhabited road, and they followed close after.

"Where do you think he's going?" Rebecca asked.

JJ blinked. "There aren't many places up this way . . . except . . . the hospital."

Rebecca's eyes widened. "Yes. That's gotta be it. That's where he's headed."

The Toyota took the first exit at the small roundabout ahead and they followed past a sign with a large *H* for hospital.

"Wonder why he ditched the Tesla," JJ said.

"I don't know." Rebecca turned into the expansive hospital parking lot and came to a stop. They followed Brenda's husband into the hospital reception area. It was hard to be entirely sure, but JJ thought he favored his right leg while he walked, seeming to struggle as he climbed the entrance stairs.

The hospital was alive with activity but Chad Jace bypassed the reception desk and made his way directly to the elevator.

They watched him enter an empty elevator but stopped short of following him inside. JJ caught a good look at him as the doors closed. He was dressed in a tight, black T-shirt beneath a dark blazer. Their eyes met for a moment. His gaze traveled down her neck as he looked her up and down. He flashed a hyena-hungry grin.

In that singular look, JJ knew precisely the sort of man he was. The sort that leaned against doorways in office breakrooms when you were eating or brushed too closely past you on a crowded subway train. *A total creep.*

The elevator door closed, but his aftershave lingered in the lobby, thick as gun smoke in the air.

Rebecca must have seen him too. "He's dressed like he's got a hot date."

JJ nodded. "A steaming hot one."

"Seventh floor," Rebecca said, pointing at the electronic floor display above the elevator.

JJ nodded as they filed into the next available elevator and pressed for the seventh floor. When they arrived, they could smell that same cologne—oak with hints of amber and sandalwood.

JJ sniffed. "He's here."

They walked down a corridor of what seemed to be private wings, doing their best to glance inside as they did so. They came at last to a ward with a half-open door, where the scent of the cologne was strongest. JJ made a casual effort to peek inside. It was only for a moment, but she saw all that she needed. Brenda's husband was kissing a bedridden woman with long golden hair. Instinctively, she turned toward the patient manifest pinned just beside the door.

JJ slipped her phone out silently. "Clearly not his wife."

Rebecca nodded, glancing at the name.

"Clerken," she muttered under her breath as she saw the name on the door. "Clerken, J."

JJ kept Rebecca moving forward, refusing to slow their speed so as not to arouse any suspicion from anyone on the floor.

"What do we do?" Rebecca said as they slipped out into the emergency stairwell.

JJ took a deep breath. "We have a name," she said, typing it into her mobile phone, "and pretty soon, we'll have a face." She frowned. On the one hand, they had enough to see that something fishy was definitely going on with Chad, but something in her stomach made her feel that it wasn't enough. Chad Jace was a creep and the mere mention of his infidelity might be insufficient for Brenda to make a decision. If this was their one opportunity to expose him, then it was worth going all out to do it. JJ cleared her throat. "Telling Brenda what we saw won't be enough for her. We need to get photographs."

Rebecca nodded. "I agree, but how do we do that? If we just walk in there, any cover we have is blown for good."

JJ blinked and pinched the bridge of her nose as her mind worked frantically on a solution.

Rebecca nodded knowingly. "Oh, no, you're making your Sherlock face."

JJ moved toward the corridor and spotted a small janitor's closet halfway down the hall. Her eyes widened as the outline of a plan started to form in her mind. "Follow me."

They crept back into the corridor and made their way into the supply closet. It had barely enough space for the two of them, but all the supplies JJ had hoped for were there: clinical facemasks, latex gloves, hospital blue overalls, and surgical caps.

Rebecca's eyes widened as JJ searched through the supplies. "Oh . . . crafty."

Moments later, JJ and Rebecca stepped out from the supply closet dressed like scrub nurses en route to surgery. JJ's heart was pounding as they walked toward the half-open hospital wing. She hoped Chad would only take a fleeting look, so they could get in and out without suspicion.

"Here we go," JJ whispered under her breath as they came at last to the room marked *Clerken, J.*

JJ knocked once and, before receiving an answer, pushed the door open in an officious haste. Chad threw his hands up in a strange attempt of defense, startled by the sudden interruption.

JJ glanced down at her phone as though double-checking information. "Mrs. Saline?"

The woman in the hospital bed leaned forward to prop herself up on her elbow. "No."

JJ gave an apologetic look. "I'm so sorry, wrong room." She held up her phone as though to verify information, bringing the camera into view. "Is this E24?"

The woman shook her head. "D24."

JJ had her in perfect frame and took the picture. To her utter horror, the phone made a loud camera shutter sound that made the entire room go still. Chad's jaw tightened with a rageful expression and for a moment, JJ froze. There was no denying that sound.

He spoke in an almost menacing growl. "Did you just take a picture of us?"

JJ just stared at him for a moment, offering no response.

Rebecca moved quickly to disrupt the silence. "E24 is the next floor up. We're sorry to bother you."

The sound of Rebecca's voice seemed to snap her out of her momentary stupor and she gave a tight-lipped smile. "I sometimes get the floors mixed up."

"Did you just take a photo of us?" Chad repeated.

JJ shook her head. "Of course not." She turned toward the door.

"Hey!" he called after them.

JJ grabbed Rebecca's arm and pulled her forward, trying to maintain a normal walking pace until they entered the corridor. Once there, JJ whispered, "Run!"

Chad stumbled out after them, but from the stuttered sound of his footsteps, it was clear that JJ had not imagined his limp earlier. He appeared to have a true injury that severely impaired his mobility.

They slammed into the door to the emergency stairwell and sprinted down the concrete steps. *There's no way he's catching us.*

They entered a corridor a few floors below and quickly discarded their disguises in a closet propped open with a bucket and mop. A loud ping announced the elevator's arrival and the door slid open. Chad Jace stood panting in the elevator. For a moment, JJ wanted to run again, but then she remembered that he'd seen only their masked faces. Running now would be a dead giveaway. JJ looked at Rebecca, and they stepped into the elevator.

Chad's crimson face showed his tense anger. JJ's heart beat like it was going to break free from her ribcage. The ride down felt like an eternity, but mercifully, they came to the ground floor and Chad's realization of their ploy never seemed to come.

"Ladies first," he said when the elevator door slid silently open.

JJ hesitated as Rebecca stepped out, then followed after. She walked out into the reception area and nodded to Rebecca, pointing toward the exit.

"Excuse me," she heard a male voice say behind them.

Her heartbeat quickened as she kept walking, not wanting to look back.

"Excuse me," the voice came again, more urgent this time.

JJ didn't slow down.

"Excuse me!"

A firm hand gripped her by the wrist. She gave a start and touched her chest as she glanced over her shoulder. It was Chad Jace. In his hand, he held out a small white card.

"You dropped this," he said, sporting a polite smile.

JJ blinked. It was her business card, one of the ones that her mother had gifted them at the restaurant earlier. With the words *Julia Kamaras, Private Detective*, written in dark bold capitals.

JJ sucked in a breath and accepted the card. "Thank you." It seemed he hadn't looked at it.

He gave her a long, suspicious look then let go of her wrist. "You're welcome."

JJ walked hastily toward the exit, motioning to Rebecca to do the same. They walked back to the car in total silence, and once safely inside, both let out almighty breaths of relief.

"That was a close one," Rebecca said.

JJ nodded, breathing hard. "Too close."

JJ jumped as her cell phone started to ring again. It was a number she didn't recognize calling from out of state. She let out a small breath, calming herself, and answered.

"Hello?"

A woman's voice sounded on the phone. "Hello?"

JJ leaned forward. "Hello, Kamaras, Brannigan, and Quinones."

"May I please speak to JJ Kamaras?"

"Yes, this is she."

"Wonderful," the woman said. "My name is Winona Dakota."

JJ instantly recognized the name and the voice. Winona Dakota had been the host of a daytime talk show called *Dakota* that had aired nationwide from the Las Vegas strip for at least a decade.

"How can I help you?" JJ asked.

"Ms. Kamaras, how would you like to spend a week in Las Vegas?"

CHAPTER 3

Brenda Jace pulled JJ into a tight hug and let out a shuddering sob. "Thank you," she whispered.

JJ gave an encouraging smile as they pulled apart. "I am so sorry this happened."

Brenda nodded. "I'm just glad I know for sure now."

For a woman who had just been given proof that her husband was having an affair, Brenda Jace seemed to be doing okay. Her husband Chad, it turned out, had been in a year-long affair with a woman called Joanne Clerken whom he'd met at a realtor function. The Toyota, the limp, and the hospital rendezvous were all explained by the fact that the two had been involved in a road accident just the week before. After a boozy dinner, Chad's Tesla had been badly damaged in a car accident. He had come out largely unscathed, but Joanne had suffered a broken leg and was recuperating in the hospital. The accident hadn't been enough to discourage them, and Chad visited her under partner status while she recovered, using his credit card to pay her hospital bills. The photographs were the icing on the top of a large, three-tiered cheater's cake.

It felt good to issue their first official invoice, knowing that they had earned the approval of their appreciative, albeit heartbroken, client.

JJ let out a breath as the car pulled out into the street and disappeared down the road.

Rebecca touched her shoulder. "Our first satisfied client."

JJ nodded. "More to come."

Rebecca smiled. "Have you decided what to do about Winona Dakota?"

JJ shrugged. "Not really."

"Winona Dakota?" Gwen Q asked. "The one who used to have the talk show back in the day?"

"That's the one. She called last night after we found Chad Jace with his mistress. She invited us all out to Las Vegas as special guests for the unveiling of a Native American sculpture at one of those fancy hotels on the strip."

"What did you tell her?" Gwen Q asked.

"I told her I'd think about it."

Gwen raised an eyebrow. "What's there to think about? An all-expense paid trip to Las Vegas? Sounds amazing."

"But we've barely gotten things settled with the agency. Maybe this isn't the right time to just up and go."

Rebecca crossed her arms in front of her. "Look, we've just solved your first big case, and the trip is just for a week. Besides, the publicity from an event like that will have the new clients racing in. Think big, JJ."

"Vegas for a week would be nice," Gwen Q added.

"More than nice," Rebecca said.

JJ rolled her eyes. Rebecca had probably packed her bags already, and asking in front of Gwen Q was just a thinly veiled attempt to ensure a majority vote. Even so, JJ had to admit that the idea of visiting Las Vegas was intriguing, as she had never been there before. And perhaps Rebecca was right about it helping, not hindering, their business. Still, she hesitated.

"Is there something we're missing?" Gwen asked, looking confused.

JJ lowered her head. "It's just . . ."

Rebecca's eyes suddenly widened with realization, and she nodded silently to herself. "Of course. Oh my gosh, JJ, I forgot."

"Yup."

"Okay, really confused over here," Gwen added.

"It's Max. He lives there now," JJ said. "Works on the Las Vegas strip, too."

"Oh, right," Gwen said, appearing to recall how strong JJ's feelings for Max had been and her disappointment when he started becoming enchanted with man-magnet rival gymnast, Priti Patel, before her untimely passing.

"It's not that it's a problem," JJ said. "Just feels a little weird. It all ended so suddenly just when it seemed like things were progressing. Plus, the whole Priti thing."

"I understand," Gwen Q said softly. "But still . . ."

"Exactly. Still . . . could be time to put it all behind you," Rebecca suggested. "But whatever you decide, we're on your team."

"No, you're right." JJ felt her decision was made. Max was no reason to run from Vegas. Clearly, they'd both moved on.

"*Soooo.*" Rebecca leaned toward JJ, wide-eyed.

"All right, I'll call her back," JJ said with a resolute nod, as a smile grew on her face. "Vegas, here we come."

JJ spent the rest of the week hard at work. Work for her was comprised of three distinct segments. The first was her detective agency which was a true expression of her desire to help people. Aunt Constanza had called her a *truth-seeker,* and in her detective work, she had found a real place to pursue that side of herself. The second part belonged to her gymnastics gym, Boundless, where she'd been coaching local teens in competitive gymnastics since returning to Jim Thorpe, though most were soon leaving the town for college with hopes of taking their gymnastics to the next level.

The third but perhaps her most beloved part was in the kitchen—especially hosting the special brunch on Sundays with her family at the Kamaras Grill. What started as a fundraiser for the regional gymnastics championships over Thanksgiving had turned into a crowd favorite, where JJ created a menu of Greek fusion dishes that had since become a staple of the Jim Thorpe dining scene. With so many irons in the fire, time had become a precious commodity. The prospect of laying it all aside for a week in sunny Vegas was a source of both excitement and anxiety.

That Sunday, with the kitchen purring at a brisk pace to keep up with an unusually busy Sunday brunch, her father Kostas appeared at her shoulder.

"Good," he said, watching her plate the burrata. "Your pitta is very soft today. Excellent work."

JJ smiled. "I added just a touch more water and flour."

He nodded. "I can tell."

Her father was a master in the kitchen himself, so he knew how territorial one could become when the dishes had your name attached to them. He walked around the counter with his arms folded and an unusually apprehensive look. JJ could tell that he had come to talk to her about something that had nothing to do with cooking.

"So . . ." he began. "Vegas, eh?"

There it is.

She turned to him and wiped her palms on her apron. "Yes, Vegas. We've been invited to the unveiling of a priceless Native American statue. Winona Dakota said she'd heard of our work." JJ could hardly believe it herself.

Kostas gave an approving nod. "Good for you. I'm glad you're being recognized around the country for your special talents."

"Thanks," JJ said. "Though I'm not really sure how my talents, as you call them, come into play at an art show."

"Well, you *are* going to a casino." Kostas smirked.

"Ha *ha*." JJ put a hand on her hip. "I don't think it's for my poker skills, Dad."

"I see." His smile waned and he looked squarely at JJ. "One thing I wanted to mention before you go."

"Okay, what?"

"Be careful out there. Las Vegas is not like Jim Thorpe. Or like

Italy." He lowered his voice. "I used to know a man . . ." He hesitated. "Things go on there."

"Yes, I'm sure, but this isn't anything serious! It's just an unveiling of a sculpture. It'll be like a vacation."

He nodded. "I know, I know. I'm just saying, danger has a way of finding you, Julia."

JJ felt a tingle of excitement as the hairs on the back of her neck rose ever so slightly. "I'll be fine, Dad."

He touched her shoulder. "Of course you will."

He scooped out a dollop of hummus with a fresh spoon, tasted it, and gave a nod of approval. "Perfect."

JJ watched him leave and turned back to the burrata. Her father always had a nose for trouble. He could tell before anyone else when it was coming. The problem, of course, was that there was that part of JJ that secretly lived for trouble.

Without knowing it, he had just removed any shadow of a doubt that this Las Vegas trip *had* to happen.

When she finished at the restaurant, she headed home, packed her suitcase, and readied herself for the trip that was to come, trouble or not.

* * *

JJ STARED down at the name on her cell phone screen and took a deep breath. It had been a long time since she'd spoken to Max. The Las Vegas Strip was a busy, frenetic place—over eighty thousand visitors a day, she'd read— but she felt maybe she owed him a heads up, just in case they bumped into each other. She started to text a message, then thought of Rebecca's words and deleted it. They had both moved on with their lives, so was it really necessary?

The captain's voice sounded on the airplane intercom, announcing that they were ready for departure. A passing flight attendant politely asked JJ to turn off her phone and handed her two elegant menu cards, one for food and the other for wine and champagne. It was the first time that JJ had ever flown first class. Winona Dakota and the

Neapolitan had really pulled out all the stops. JJ glanced down at the menu with interest as the sound of the airplane engine rose.

"I could get used to this," Rebecca said with a grin from the seat beside her. She pushed a button on the side of her seat, delighting in the discovery that her chair reclined into nearly a full-length bed. "We'll save that for later."

"Champagne?" the air hostess asked them.

Rebecca nodded as JJ smiled wide. "Yes, please."

"And you, miss?" the attendant asked, turning to Gwen Q, who was seated across the aisle. She gave an emphatic nod.

The flight attendant returned with three glasses of champagne in beautiful crystal stemware.

Gwen had already won the attention of a sophisticated business type in the window seat who had just loosened his tie. She held up her champagne flute toward her friends and flashed a smile. "Cheers, girls."

But that was just the beginning. First came a delectable amuse-bouche course—small bites of goat cheese crusted with crushed pistachio, prosciutto with truffled burrata, and scallop tartare. For her main course, JJ opted for a vegetable tortellini with basil cream sauce, braised lamb, and wild mushrooms. Next to her, Rebecca had treated herself to beluga caviar and the broiled lobster with herbed butter, while Gwen chose the lobster and a creamy asparagus side.

As she ate, JJ felt increasingly sure about her decision to come. It felt liberating to just enjoy a trip away with no strings attached.

The time seemed to fly by, and before JJ had managed a few winks of sleep in her luxuriously reclined chair, they arrived at Harry Reid International Airport. The flight deck intercom came alive and the captain's voice filled the cabin. "Ladies and gentlemen, welcome to Las Vegas, Nevada."

Rebecca exhaled an audible, slow gush.

Gwen Q leaned across the aisle and grinned. "We're here."

Free from all apprehension now, JJ felt excited in a way she hadn't been in a long time. Here she was in Las Vegas with her best friends in the world, and the only thing they'd been asked to do was to enjoy themselves. Rebecca, always seeming to read her mind, touched her hand and whispered, "You deserve this."

The seatbelt sign went off and they all rose to their feet.

The flight attendant stood by the door and gave them a star-bright smile as they walked past. "Thank you for flying with us."

"Thank *you*," JJ said, turning toward the door.

They were told at baggage claim that their luggage had been transferred directly to "Ms. Kamaras's chauffeur in the arrivals terminal."

"*Chauffeur*," Rebecca said with an impressed look.

"You're a good person to know, Ms. Kamaras," Gwen Q added with a chuckle.

A tall, thin, dark-haired man stood at the center of the arrivals terminal with a sign that read *Kamaras, Brannigan, and Quinones* in scraggly block capitals. He was dressed in a black uniform with a golden insignia that read *The Neapolitan*.

They locked eyes with him and he greeted them with a warm smile.

"Good afternoon, ladies, and welcome to Las Vegas. My name is Noah, and I'll be driving you throughout your stay with us at the Neapolitan."

"Good afternoon, Noah." JJ tried to be composed but smiled uncontrollably. "It's really good to be here."

CHAPTER 4

Their car, a dark-tinted Lincoln Navigator, was parked in a premium space reserved for the Neapolitan just a few strides from the door outside the arrivals terminal. Noah opened the passenger door and they climbed inside, finding a champagne bucket on ice with three long-stem glasses and a box of butter caramel cookies.

Soft jazz played as the car pulled out of the airport parking lot. Less than a half hour later, the towering buildings and bright lights of downtown Las Vegas seemed to crowd around their car like gaudy spectators.

"This is the Las Vegas Strip," Noah said, lowering the music. "That's the Venetian," he said pointing to his right. "Over there is the Aquarium and further down is the Bellagio." They drove down for a little while before Noah spoke again. "Over there is the Golden Penny," he said with a look that JJ thought was a little disdainful. "And last but most certainly not least, our destination—the Neapolitan. Welcome to the best hotel on the Las Vegas Strip." He pulled into the hotel VIP area.

When Noah drove around to the entranceway, two dapper porters approached the car. They removed the women's luggage with perfectly choreographed steps while a third porter stepped up to escort them inside.

"Here's my card," Noah offered. "Just call me when you need a ride, and I'll be here to take you wherever you need to go."

"Thank you, Noah," JJ said, collecting the card.

They were ushered into the hotel, passing underneath a large banner that read *Welcome to the WIPB*.

"What's the WIPB?" Gwen Q asked.

JJ shrugged. "No clue."

They approached the front desk where a bespectacled receptionist in a maroon skirt suit smiled up at them. "Welcome to the Neapolitan. Are you here for the WIPB?"

JJ shook her head. "No, we aren't."

The receptionist nodded, typing something into her laptop. "May I take your names, please?"

JJ leaned over the counter. "Julia Kamaras, Rebecca Brannigan, and Gwen Quinones."

The receptionist's eyes widened. "Oh, of course, you're guests of Miss Dakota."

JJ nodded. "That's right."

The receptionist smiled. "You're in our Royal Suite. You will absolutely love it. Miss Dakota will meet you up there shortly."

She handed them a stack of key cards and gestured to the porter. "Enjoy your stay."

The Royal Suite was on one of the uppermost floors of the Neapolitan and had three en suite bedrooms, a powder room, wet bar, full-size dining table, living room, and balcony behind remote controlled shades. On the dining table sat a chocolate bouquet, yet another ice bucket of champagne, and a cheese board.

"I've seen more champagne in the last six hours than in my entire life," Gwen Q said.

Rebecca laughed. "This place is . . ."

"Stunning." It was the only word JJ could use to describe it. And their home for a week.

A doorbell rang and the trio turned to face it.

"I'll get it," Rebecca said, stepping up.

She glanced through the peephole and pulled the door open. A lovely, radiant woman stepped inside. Her straight, dark hair shimmered in the light and fell past her shoulders onto her aqua-hued, tailored dress.

"Hello, ladies." Winona Dakota locked eyes with JJ and grinned. "Welcome to Las Vegas."

Rebecca gently closed the door. "You were always my favorite talk show host. Well, after Barbara Walters."

Winona chucked and touched her chest. "I appreciate that. We're so glad to have you all here. I'm the general manager now. After I retired from the show, I decided to go into the business end of the hotel, but my first love has always been media and the arts. When I heard about everything that happened with you three in Italy, and then discovered your work in Jim Thorpe, I spoke to the Board of Directors, and we all agreed you would be the perfect guests to unveil the Arapaho. Smart and fearless women."

"Wow, thank you," JJ said, as Gwen nodded.

"It's really an honor," Rebecca added.

Winona flashed that Hollywood smile again and turned to JJ. "And I know you're quite the chef, Miss Kamaras. You'll be pleased to know that there are eight restaurants in the Neapolitan, each with distinct cuisine and menus. We have a twenty-four-hour bar on the ground floor and of course, we have the very best casino in Las Vegas across three basement floors." She smiled at JJ. "I've heard you quite enjoy a game of poker."

JJ gave a small nod. "I do."

Winona reached into her blazer pocket. "I hope you're fans of Slade Stone because we arranged tickets to his opening show tonight on the first floor. It starts at nine, so you can go just after dinner if you would like to."

"I love Slade Stone," Gwen Q announced.

Winona, hardly skipping a beat, handed them over a credit card marked with the Neapolitan logo. "The security pin is your room number. You can change it to anything you like. You can charge expenses on the card up to five thousand dollars, but if you have more expenses for any reason at all, just let me know, and I'm sure we would be able to help."

Rebecca smiled. "I think I like you more than Barbara Walters now."

They all laughed.

"The sculpture unveiling takes place tomorrow afternoon, so until then, you have the freedom to enjoy all the hotel amenities and everything else that Las Vegas has to offer." She held out a business card. "My cell number in case you need anything in the meantime."

JJ inspected the card with a quick glance. *Winona Dakota, General Manager, The Neapolitan Hotel and Casino.*

JJ slid the card into her pocket. "Thank you so much, Winona."

"Is there anything you'd like to know before I go?"

After a brief pause, JJ spoke up. "There is one thing. What restaurant would you recommend for our first night in Vegas?"

Winona grinned. "My personal favorite—Ishin. It's a Japanese steakhouse on the fourth floor. Perfect for a group and sure to set the right tone before a Slade Stone concert. I can have the reception desk book you a table, if you would like?"

They all nodded their agreement.

"Absolutely," Gwen Q confirmed.

"Seven o'clock?"

JJ nodded. "Perfect."

* * *

THEY SPENT the rest of the afternoon exploring the vast hotel which, as Gwen Q pointed out, was more like its own city. Gwen jumped at an opportunity for a hot stone massage at the hotel spa and Rebecca called Noah to request a driving tour of the city. JJ found herself wandering around taking full inventory of the hotel—the medical center, the swimming pool, the eight restaurants that Winona had mentioned, and more. For some reason, habit probably, she found herself noticing their camera surveillance system in each area. Her final stop was at the hotel auditorium that would soon play host to Slade Stone and a crowd of several thousand. A giant poster image of the rock star guitarist dominated the entrance to the auditorium, featuring Stone with his guitar raised aloft as though offering a sacrifice to the great gods of rock and roll. JJ's mind drifted to the last time she had been at a public music performance—the night the maestro Vito Natale was killed. This time she would have her eyes peeled for anything suspicious.

The trio reconvened at the hotel suite just in time for dinner, with JJ being the last to arrive. Gwen Q, who was never one to be effusive with praise, gushed openly about the quality of the spa and the care taken by each member of the staff. Rebecca spoke in similar terms of her day out with Noah, noting the rich local culture that she encountered just off the Las Vegas strip.

Dressed and ready for their first night out in Vegas, they left their palatial suite and headed for Ishin. JJ loved experiencing all types of food but had to admit when it came to Japanese cuisine, she was a true novice. The restaurant's façade was a palette of blacks, reds, and pale blues across a wide panel of glass. Inside, the main dining room was guarded by a half-wall of blond wood and lattice screens. The woman who stepped forward to greet them was shockingly beautiful and poised. Vegas appeared to have its own magnetic appeal that attracted the most talented and attractive staff—the cream of the crop.

JJ tried not to stare, but it was impossible in the face of such an example of near-human perfection. No surgeon could have carved better cheekbones or artist painted more perfect features. Her straight black hair fell beyond her shoulders with a gleam reminiscent of fresh ink. She greeted the trio with a tranquil smile that showed a row of perfect white teeth.

"Welcome to Ishin," the woman said with a voice that carried the faintest trace of a Japanese accent. "Do you have a reservation?"

JJ closed her mouth and gathered herself, half deciding if the slight accent was real or whether, like so much of Las Vegas, a near-perfect approximation and clever business tactic designed to create a feeling of authenticity. *No, you're being cynical.*

"Yes," JJ answered. "Seven o'clock, Kamaras, Brannigan—"

"And Quinones," the woman finished with a smile.

"That's right."

Her smile widened. "I'll show you to your table."

For all its outward flamboyance, the interior of Ishin was refreshingly minimal. Adopting a classic Japanese style, Ishin's main dining room featured plain wooden tables, a flower display near the entrance and nice quality white linen napkins. They were seated at a lovely, small table close to the center of the restaurant.

JJ looked for the little signs of excellence that were always present in a good restaurant. The watchful vigilance of waiters and waitresses. The ceaseless movement of the hostess and managing staff. The sound of hissing, steaming, and simmering whenever the kitchen door opened. The faint aroma of something delicious in the air. All the signs were there. She felt her body relax. *This is going to be good.*

Their order was the perfect balance between the familiar and the adventurous. Sake, sushi, and sashimi were all featured but so were chicken, beef, and pork. Just as their main course was cleared away, JJ spotted a vaguely familiar figure seated across the room—a heavy-set man with only half a head of gray hair. His clasped hands featured glistening gold rings and a thick, heavy-linked watch. His smile to the waitress revealed a diamond-encrusted incisor.

Rebecca noticed him too. "That's . . ."

"Bruce," JJ confirmed. "Bruce Balvin."

Their eyes met from across the room and his lips curled into a deep grin. JJ's heartbeat quickened as she held his stare. Bruce Balvin was a hard man whose position as the kingmaker of the online sports betting space in Jim Thorpe had put him at the hub of criminal activity in Pennsylvania and beyond. *What is he doing here?*

JJ rose to her feet.

Rebecca tugged at JJ's clothes and whispered forcefully. "What are you doing?"

"Seeing what he's doing here," she said taking a step toward him.

Just then, a large group of suited corporate types impeded her vision as they sauntered by. Through the crowd of people, she saw Bruce Balvin motion for the check.

Oh, no, you don't!

JJ pushed through the throng of people as politely as she could muster. She arrived at his table, but Bruce was nearly out of sight and heading toward the exit. She quickened her step to catch him, but when she emerged from behind the wood-paneled half-wall, he was gone.

She glanced at the beautiful hostess who had seen them to their table. "Did you see where . . ." She sighed in defeat. "Never mind."

What could she possibly say? For all she knew, Bruce Balvin was here for a vacation just like she was. What would she even say if she caught up with him? *You are not here for work,* she reminded herself.

With that, she returned to her seat. *I'm just going to forget about it and enjoy my dinner.*

Yeah, who was she kidding.

CHAPTER 5

Rebecca and Gwen Q were not nearly as worried about Bruce Balvin as JJ was. Their reasoning made perfect sense, both of them insisting it was perfectly logical for a bookmaker —criminal or otherwise—to be vacationing in Las Vegas, the holy land of gambling. Though JJ knew that this explanation was entirely possible, something told her that it was just too good to be true. Of all the hotels on the strip, why was Bruce Balvin there? Why now? One thing JJ knew for sure about Balvin—if there was big money to be made, he'd find his way right into the shady middle of the action. She tried to put the thought out of her mind and focus on the night ahead. *I'm not here to work.*

A tall, slim, elegantly dressed man approached the table with the air of proprietary confidence that was the exclusive domain of the cultured elite and shamefully rich. JJ felt sure no velvet rope nor bullish bouncer had ever barred his entry to anything. He walked right up to their table and stood with his head held high.

"Good evening, ladies. I hope you are enjoying your evening."

"Yes, we are, thank you," JJ offered, giving the man an appraising gaze.

He smiled. "My name is Montell Cooper." He said the name with a declaratory slant, as though it was a name they ought to have immediately recognized. He waited a moment, plainly saddened that no one had known. "I am the Operations Director of the Neapolitan."

The three women smiled, and in succession, expressed to him their delight and gratitude for being there.

"Glad everything has been to your liking so far. If you need anything at all, you can call the reception desk and ask for me. I'll be happy to help any way I can."

With that, he was gone.

The Slade Stone concert was more fun than JJ had had in a long time, and after two-plus hours of dancing in the aisles and belting out songs along with the rocker, they all left with an air of electric delight. They made their way into the main lobby and stood near the elevators.

Despite the late hour, or perhaps because of it, the Neapolitan was still abuzz with activity. Two men were seated at the edge of the hotel lobby deep in discussion. Though they sat facing away from her, something about the men provoked a strange feeling of familiarity in JJ.

"What is it?" Gwen Q asked, staring at JJ.

Rebecca leaned forward. "Oh, no. She has the look."

JJ narrowed her eyes and continued to stare at the men before turning back to her friends. "It's nothing."

JJ went to press the elevator button going up, but Rebecca blocked her hand.

"You have *got* to be joking if you think we're going to bed right now."

JJ glanced at her watch. "It's almost midnight."

"And we're in Las Vegas. The city that never sleeps."

"I thought that was New York," Gwen Q said.

"It's both," Rebecca said.

"So, what do you want to do instead?" JJ asked.

Rebecca grinned and pushed the button going down. "The casino."

JJ's eyebrows rose. With all of the day's activity, she had almost forgotten that there was a massive casino right here with endless gambling and entertainment possibilities.

They stepped into the elevator and just as the doors were sliding closed, one of the two men sitting in the hotel lobby turned toward JJ.

A bolt of electric current flashed through her.

It couldn't be.

CHAPTER 6

Tim Ream.

He clearly noticed her as well and raised a wine glass in salute, grinning widely. His companion turned around.

Another alarm sounded in JJ's head.

Johnny Golden.

Rebecca craned her neck in the men's direction. "Hey, that looks like—"

The elevator door closed. JJ rushed to press the *open* button but the elevator was already on the move.

JJ turned to Rebecca. "You saw them, too."

Rebecca gave her an uncertain look. "I'm not sure what I saw. Let's just go have some fun, okay?"

"Saw what?" Gwen looked confused.

"The two men in the lobby," JJ said. "I'm telling you, it was Tim Ream and Johnny Golden."

"Here?" Gwen was taken aback.

"Yes," JJ snapped.

"You're sure?" Gwen asked, then turned to Rebecca. "And you saw them too?"

"Well, I don't know . . ." Rebecca shook her head.

"Yes." JJ nodded. "We saw them. I'm sure."

She tapped the G button repeatedly to take them back to the ground floor, but the elevator had other instructions to answer first.

"JJ," Rebecca said, touching her arm. "So maybe it was them, but we're not here for all that. Can we just enjoy our time here, please?"

The elevator door slid open on the casino floor and the sounds of excitement, despair, and chiming slot machines filled her ears.

"Please," Rebecca said again, with a pleading look.

JJ lowered her head and let out a resigned sigh. "Of course. You're right. We're not here for work."

They stepped out into the casino. JJ started to wonder if there was a chance she had only imagined seeing Tim Ream. Perhaps it was the casino atmosphere. Maybe part of her unconsciously wanted to throw some chaos into the mix. Seeing three Elvises stroll by, she acknowledged the possibility that it was just a look-a-like. She shook her head as though to drive the thought from her mind and fixed her gaze ahead to the gambling floor.

JJ's phone rang in her pocket. Constanza's name appeared across the screen.

"Be back in a sec," JJ said, stepping toward the bathroom in search of some quiet. "I'll catch up with you guys."

"Ciao, Constanza," she said, answering the phone.

"Ciao, my dear! How's Las Vegas treating you? Rita sent me the news report about your being invited there by a TV celebrity. Impressive."

JJ smiled. "So far, so good."

"Then why do you sound so stressed, bella?"

JJ hesitated. Her story might sound crazy. *No, Constanza will understand.* "I seem to be seeing faces from the past. Dangerous faces. Faces that don't like me very much. But I'm not fully sure."

"How many of these faces?"

"Three so far."

The line went quiet and the silence extended so long that JJ had to check that they were still connected. "Constanza?"

"I'm still here."

"What is it?" JJ asked.

"How sure are you?"

"Pretty positive. They seemed to recognize me, too."

Constanza gave a low groan. "Be careful out there. Many years ago, when I was still working with the police, two men who I had arrested met in prison and put a plan together for when they were released. Tried to get me stuck in a burning building."

"How did you stop them?" JJ asked.

"I thought I saw one of them in the parking lot. I wasn't sure. But I decided to take the stairs instead of the elevator. It saved my life."

"You think they're here to hurt me?"

"No, not necessarily. It might just be pure coincidence and have nothing at all to do with you. Just stay sharp. And remember, a shared enemy binds bad people together better than glue."

"Right." JJ nodded. "I'll keep my eyes open."

"You do that."

"How are things in Italy?"

"Picking up," Constanza said. "Bello and I have been hired for a couple new murder investigations, real head-scratchers."

JJ smiled, remembering the aging chocolate Labrador retriever that was Constanza's dearest companion. "We'll have to talk again when we have more time. I want details."

"That's a deal," Constanza said. "Next trip, I'll come to see you. It has been a while since I visited America."

"That would be really nice. I'd love you to meet my family and come to our restaurant."

"Sounds wonderful. Look, I'm going to let you go, but you be careful. And don't second guess yourself. You have superb instincts. Trust your gut."

"Thank you. I will." JJ felt emboldened by the seasoned detective's advice and words of encouragement. "Okay, I'll talk to you soon, Constanza."

JJ returned to the gambling floor and found Rebecca and Gwen Q at the roulette table. They gave her a hundred dollar's worth of chips, and she joined at the next turn, placing ten dollars on the number seventeen black and five dollars on seventeen red. The waistcoated croupier gave the roulette wheel a furious spin, and the little ball began its sojourn in the opposite direction.

At last, the wheel came to a tittering stop and the croupier's eyes widened. "Black seventeen," he announced.

Rebecca gave JJ a quiet applause as the croupier paid out the winnings in chips.

"Good start," came a voice from behind them.

JJ, Rebecca, and Gwen all turned at once. The debonaire man standing right behind them wore a dark tuxedo and stood with a martini in his hand. Another familiar face. Luckily, this time, a friendly one.

Bond007forlife.

JJ threw back her head and laughed. "Is everyone I've ever known in Vegas this week?"

The man took a small sip from his martini glass and grinned. His real name was Daniel Krug, but after years of knowing him only by his online cardroom name, Bond007forlife just stuck. "Where else would the gamblers be at a time like this?"

JJ gave him a confused look. "What do you mean?"

"The World International Poker Bowl is being hosted here at the Neapolitan. All the very best poker players worldwide are here to play. Two-million-dollar prize pot."

JJ's eyebrows rose. "The WIPB," she mumbled. *World International Poker Bowl.* That was what all the signs were for. That's why Tim Ream, Johnny Golden, and even Bruce Balvin were there. If a high roller table in little Jim Thorpe could draw their attention, surely an event like this one would.

"That explains it," JJ said. "I almost thought I was seeing things."

"I assumed the WIPB was why *you* were here, too," Bond007forlife said.

JJ shook her head. "I'm here for the unveiling of the Arapaho."

"What's that?"

"It's a Native American sculpture. Newly recovered and unveiled for the very first time for public exhibition."

Bond007forlife gave an impressed look. "I see. An art show." He finished the rest of his martini and glanced across the casino at the high roller table. "So, I guess that means no poker for you, then?"

JJ gave a confident, feral smile. "Oh, no, my friend. Bring it on."

CHAPTER 7

The screech of her phone alarm from the bedside table caused JJ to sit up with a jolt. She let out an exasperated groan as she turned onto her side and tapped the snooze button. Just a few more precious minutes of sleep and she would be good to go.

The second time the alarm went off, she slowly climbed out of bed. The poker game the night before had run on until the early hours of the morning, with her wine glass mysteriously being continually replenished without her doing. Mercifully, she had no hangover, though her ears still throbbed from the thump of the speakers that had incessantly blasted music just behind their poker table all night.

The unveiling of the Arapaho was just a few hours away. JJ got dressed slowly, taking her time to put her outfit together. Rita Natale had reminded them that the Arapaho unveiling could represent a substantial photo op for their new detective agency and insisted that the dress JJ had initially intended to wear was too simple—she needed one that would "scream Las Vegas." The outfit they had both decided upon was a dazzling lime green tailored pantsuit that was glitzy and chic, yet still professional.

Rebecca was wearing a sleek, designer silk dress that instantly gained Rita's stamp of approval. They smiled at one another as they convened in the suite's living room. Gwen Q was the last to arrive. She'd opted for her own unique look, as always, and somehow managed to pull off a superstar quality. Today was no exception. Her bronze ringlets fell in a voluminous cascade atop her orange sherbet plunge-neck dress—a clear show-stopper that somehow also managed to look very classy.

"See, now how does she do that?" Rebecca asked JJ.

"Just the Q factor." JJ shrugged.

The suite's phone rang and Rebecca turned to answer it. JJ heard the faint hum of another voice on the line as she waited for the update.

"Okay. Sounds good. I'll ask and get back to you," Rebecca said.

Gwen Q raised a questioning eyebrow.

"It was a call from the reception desk. Winona Dakota is inviting us to take a sneak peek at the sculpture in the hotel museum just before the grand unveiling. Should we go?" Rebecca asked.

JJ and Gwen Q gave a resounding, "Yes!"

They took the elevator down to the museum floor where a few photographers were already setting up for the unveiling. The stunning hostess from the Japanese restaurant the night before stood at the museum's front desk.

"There you are," the hostess said. "Miss Dakota is waiting just this way."

She escorted them into one of the museum back rooms and closed the door behind them.

Winona Dakota stood with her back to them and glanced over her shoulder at the sound of the door closing. "Welcome." She turned back toward what was presumably the sculpture.

The hostess gestured for them to move forward and they joined Winona. JJ, Rebecca, and Gwen stood wide-eyed at the sight.

The sculpture was of a woman dressed in the full ceremonial garb of a Native American tribeswoman, cut from immaculate white stone. Her eyes were lidded with an expression that JJ read as deep contemplation and her arms were folded in front of her. Her headband was comprised of delicate bird feathers, giving her the appearance of a great princess.

"The Arapaho," Winona announced. "It is one of the most sought-after pieces in all of the world. It went missing at some point in the forties—thought to be lost in a fire. Finally, when it was recovered decades later, it took years to be restored to its full glory." She paused and her facial expression showed a sense of awe. "And now here it is. A priceless work of art."

JJ was never one to fawn over art, but it was hard to deny that there was something incredibly compelling about the Arapaho sculpture. It wasn't the size. She'd expected it to be much larger, but it was only about a foot tall. Still, an aura of power and grandeur seemed to emanate from it.

"Having this in our museum will be a game-changer for the Neapolitan."

"We're so honored to be part of the unveiling," JJ said.

Winona turned to them. "It's going to be a great day." She glanced down at her watch. "I just wanted you all to see it first. Before the cameras do."

"Thank you," Rebecca said as JJ and Gwen smiled. "This is a really special moment."

Winona Dakota drew in a breath. "We have a few hours until show time. I'd love you to meet me in my hotel room about an hour before we begin. How does that sound?"

JJ looked at her friends who gave an approving nod. "We'd love to."

"Wonderful." Winona slowly returned the Arapaho to its black case lined with purple velvet and shut the lid tight. She took the case by the sturdy handle with great care. "I'll see you soon."

Outside, the trio was rejoined by the hostess from Ishin who introduced herself as Simone. She offered them a free tour of the museum.

JJ was pensive for a moment. "Is it me, or did Winona seem strangely emotional to you?"

Rebecca nodded. "A little. But maybe that's not so weird. It seems the sculpture means a lot to her."

"I noticed it, too," Gwen Q said.

Simone glanced over her shoulder. "Miss Dakota has been working on this unveiling for almost two years. It's huge for her."

Simone told them additional details about the Neapolitan and its history as she took them through the museum. It turned out that she was the hotel's hospitality coordinator and worked in several capacities in various parts of the building. They settled in the small museum café where they talked more about the hotel over coffee. From her description, it was clear that Winona, Montell, the Operations Director they'd met earlier, and Simone were the holy trinity of the Neapolitan's management, in that order.

"Almost time to meet Winona," JJ said, glancing at her watch.

"I need to grab something from the room first," Rebecca said.

"Same here," Gwen added.

"Okay, I'll head that way and meet you there. I don't want us to be late." JJ slowly made her way to the elevator and headed up to Winona's room. When the doors opened, she stepped out into the corridor and nearly crashed into a slender man with a thick handlebar mustache and a baseball cap. JJ fell sideways in her attempt to avoid a collision and stumbled face-first onto the corridor's plush red carpet.

Waiting for an *excuse me* that never came, the handlebar mustache jerk glanced at her a brief microsecond and pushed into the elevator, tugging at his baseball cap and pulling it over his brow.

"Watch where you're going," JJ said with a scowl.

He turned away from her without response, still holding the brim of his hat, as the elevator door closed.

Gathering herself and brushing down her brand-new suit, JJ looked up to the posted signs indicating the direction of the room numbers. She turned right and followed the wide hallway until she came to Winona's room. She knocked once and the door swished silently open. It had been left ajar.

"Hello? Winona, it's me, JJ. Your door's open. Okay to come in?"

She waited a long moment but there was no answer.

"Winona?" she called again, leaning forward to peek into the room. She caught sight of a single high-heeled leg dangling over the edge of the bed, and a haunting feeling came over her. *No, she's probably just asleep.*

JJ glanced down at her watch. It was getting close to the time for the unveiling. She'd better wake Winona up.

"Winona," she called more urgently as she gently pushed the door open and walked toward the bed. The room was strangely cool and smelled of chemicals as if it had just been cleaned.

JJ narrowed her eyes and touched her knee. "Winona."

Still, no movement.

JJ's heartbeat quickened. "Winona." She frantically checked for a pulse. She waited for a moment in agonizing silence. *No pulse.*

She leaped over the bed to the hotel phone and dialed the front desk.

"Front desk," came the response.

"I need a doctor in room 7311. Winona Dakota isn't breathing. That's room 7311. I need help now!"

The receptionist answered in a panic. "7311. I'm sending the doctor up now!"

JJ slammed the phone down and shook her shoulder. "Winona!" Again, there was no response. A sick feeling grew in JJ's stomach. She stared at Winona's motionless body and staggered back. "This can't be happening. Not again."

Each second seemed an eternity as she waited for help to arrive. Finally, a man wearing a blue polo shirt ran into the room. In his left hand, he had a good-sized medical bag, in his right, a walkie-talkie.

"Are you the doctor?" JJ asked.

He nodded as he moved over to Winona's body. "Yes, I am. Do you know what happened?"

"No. I was supposed to meet her. The door was open and I found her like this."

Expertly, he checked for a pulse while grabbing a compartmented case of instruments from his bag. Confirming she had no pulse, he fanned out the contents of the case and pulled out a small syringe.

He spoke into the walkie-talkie. "We need an ambulance. No pulse, and she isn't breathing. I'm going to administer emergency protocol. Hurry."

He was emphatic, but there was a note of warm calm in his voice. Clearly, he'd seen it all before in Vegas hotel rooms. Though he was looking directly at what could have been a corpse, the doctor worked methodically and with sharp precision.

JJ watched in total silence as the doctor tried to revive her. Nothing he did showed any sign of success. She started to feel woozy and leaned on the dresser to steady herself.

A siren sounded from outside—medical services had arrived. The sound of hurried footsteps in the corridor preceded the appearance of two burly men in bright yellow emergency medical uniforms. The doctor glanced over at them and slowly shook his head.

JJ's stomach fell. She had known from the moment she had seen the leg, but now there was confirmation. Winona Dakota was presumed dead.

Her jaw tightened as she stepped away from the bed, trying to replay in her mind the moments that had just passed in her mind. She recalled the face of the man with the handlebar mustache who had collided with her at the elevator. Was he coming from Winona's corridor or from the other way?

She couldn't be sure. Just then a realization hit her smack in the face. Winona had taken the Arapaho with her up to the room. She glanced over for any sign of the dark case that she knew held the sculpture. There it was, just at the corner of the bed. She reached toward it and unlocked the latch.

It fell open.

Empty.

Her heart sank.

Her mind buzzed ferociously as she tried to remember if the man with the handlebar mustache had anything in his hands. Her mind came up blank. She simply could not remember if he was carrying anything.

She looked around the room, taking inventory of everything she could see, realizing as she moved that this could be her one clean opportunity to get a good look at what might be the scene of a crime. Perhaps even the scene of a murder. Discreetly, she studied the room, taking mental pictures of everything she saw. The open bottles of facial wash and the still-wet oatmeal cleansing bar around the bathroom sink. The discarded white sneakers beside the bedside dresser. The fact the air conditioner was off despite the room still being unnaturally cool. The scent of the cleaning supplies.

The emergency medical workers wasted no time putting Winona on a stretcher. Out in the corridor, JJ watched a distraught Montell approach the room. When he saw Winona on the stretcher, he almost collapsed in apparent shock.

"Oh no," he gasped, covering his mouth.

"Please clear the corridor," one of the emergency service workers shouted as they pushed the stretcher forcefully toward the elevator.

They quickly bundled inside and were on their way. A mere second later the other elevator door opened. Gwen Q and Rebecca, dressed for the unveiling, stepped out into the corridor. Seeing the worried look on JJ's face, they rushed toward her.

"What happened?" Rebecca said. "Are you okay?"

"I don't know." She stared blankly toward the elevator that had taken Winona's lifeless body. "I think Winona Dakota is dead."

CHAPTER 8

The press and media personnel that had arrived for the unveiling of the Arapaho had now turned their attention in another direction entirely. The Arapaho was gone and famed television talk show host Winona Dakota was feared dead.

Police arrived moments after Winona was taken away and cordoned off the entire floor. JJ was questioned by a polite yet stoic police officer who introduced herself as Officer Tyrell. The officer was laser-focused in her interview style, asking each question in a way to elicit pinpoint accuracy. JJ recounted her experience from the moment she stepped out of the elevator, making sure to give as detailed a description of the man with the handlebar mustache as she could manage. Just as Officer Tyrell was finishing her questioning, another officer stepped up to whisper something into Tyrell's ear. She became still as she listened, looking over at JJ again as though seeing her for the very first time.

The officer straightened. "What did you say your name was again, ma'am?"

"Julia Kamaras."

Officer Tyrell gave a knowing nod. "It's you, isn't it? You're the person from Pennsylvania who made a fool out of the local cops down there. Twice."

JJ wanted to protest but didn't know how. Strictly speaking, Officer Tyrell had not said anything untrue.

"I didn't make a fool out of them," JJ muttered.

Tyrell looked unconvinced, and her expression clearly showed distaste. "Tell me again how you found Miss Dakota."

JJ spoke slowly and clearly. "We were supposed to meet half an hour before the unveiling. I knocked on her door and discovered it was open. She didn't answer when I called out to her so I peeked inside and saw her leg. I thought she was asleep, so I stepped inside to wake her up for the sculpture unveiling. Then I discovered she wasn't breathing and called for help from the room phone. I waited for the doctor, and then he and emergency services arrived."

Officer Tyrell furrowed her brow. "How long were you alone with Miss Dakota?"

JJ frowned at the officer's tone. "Two minutes, maybe three at the very most. The doctor arrived quickly. The medical center is just on the floor below."

Her eyes widened. "You've been to the medical center before today?"

"Just when I was looking around."

Tyrell made a low noise at the back of her throat. "I see," she said, writing something down on her tablet. "Miss Kamaras, I am going to need you to remain on the premises until further notice. We might have more questions and will need you to respond quickly, if so."

"Of course." JJ handed the officer one of her business cards. "I'll be here if you have any more questions."

The officer rolled her eyes as she read the card. "Detective agency? Do you have any education or official qualifications for this type of work?"

JJ met her gaze. "There are no official degrees required after a high school diploma in the U.S. But I have my provisional license and a good deal of experience."

Tyrell gave a scornful look. "So, no qualifications. Noted. Stay out of our way, Miss Kamaras. This isn't Hicksville, Pennsylvania."

JJ bit her tongue and turned to Gwen Q and Rebecca who sat waiting beside the ornamental clock near the elevator.

"Are you okay?" Rebecca asked.

JJ nodded. "Let's go somewhere we can talk."

"The café at the museum," Rebecca offered. "Seems like the only place that isn't busy at this hotel."

They all agreed and Gwen Q pushed the button going down.

As Rebecca had guessed, the museum café was empty. Luckily, the twenty-something waitress/barista/cashier seemed more preoccupied with scrolling through her social media than eavesdropping on their conversation. Even so, they spoke in hushed tones.

"What do you think happened?" Gwen Q asked when they had all been served their coffee.

JJ rolled her shoulders. "I think the Arapaho was stolen, and Winona was killed in the process."

"A premeditated murder or a robbery gone wrong?" Rebecca asked.

"I'm not sure," JJ said. "There don't seem to be any obvious signs of use of violence or forced entry. Could be a meticulous killer, a careless robber, or an opportunist who saw her door open and grabbed what he could find. But we don't know for sure if she's dead. And if so, we have no idea what the cause of death might be."

"A lot of unanswered questions," Rebecca said, taking a sip from her coffee cup.

JJ nodded. "The man I saw, the one with the mustache. He seemed in a hurry. Nearly knocked me over as he went to get into the elevator."

"You think he's the person responsible?"

"That's the first place *I* would look," JJ said.

"Hmm, so what do we do?" Gwen Q asked. "Get on the case here? Catch a flight back to Jim Thorpe? Try to enjoy what's left of our trip?"

"The police are on it," JJ said. "They have better resources than we do. More staff. More experience."

"As if that's stopped us before," Gwen Q said with a smirk.

"We don't even know if there is a case to solve," JJ protested, fighting back a growing smile.

"But if there is . . ." Gwen Q said.

"A few hours ago, you guys were insisting no work in Las Vegas. You've changed your tune."

"Circumstances have changed," Rebecca urged, "and we knew this woman. She was kind to us. She went out of her way to invite us here with all expenses paid because she believed that what we do and stand for matters. We can't just leave."

"I agree," Gwen said. "We can't."

JJ agreed but still felt uneasy inserting themselves where they had no true personal stake, in addition to clearly being unwanted. "In Jim Thorpe, we had personal reasons to investigate. In Italy, Tony and Constanza directly asked us to help. This one, I'm just not sure."

The sound of the door slapping against the wall made them all turn toward the café entrance. Montell entered and walked over to their table.

"Do you mind if I speak with you ladies for a moment?" he asked.

JJ nodded. "Of course."

He pulled out a seat at the table and sat down, wringing his hands. "I need you."

"Need us?" JJ's eyes widened.

"The Arapaho is priceless. We worked for almost two years to get it here. We have to find it, and not only do you three know what it looks like, your detective skills are legendary. You must have an excellent marketing team."

Go, Rita!

"I need a team willing to go to all the places the police won't," he continued. "A team that can find the Arapaho before it gets out in the open markets. If we don't jump on this quickly, who knows if the Arapaho will ever be seen again. They may find it a decade from now in some Vegas drug lord's desert mansion."

JJ frowned. "That would be terrible."

"Yes, unthinkable. Winona's the most noble and generous woman I've ever met. Believed in the higher calling of art, of beauty. It wasn't for sale. She'd even arranged any proceeds from the unveiling to support local Vegas charities and promote the arts in schools." He started to speak but then hesitated as if unable to continue. He took a deep breath. "I know it's possible Winona may be gone, but the Arapaho is still out there. The Neapolitan is willing to pay you five hundred thousand dollars to get it back."

Rebecca pinched JJ hard under the table.

Gwen Q straightened in her chair and gulped. JJ sat composed, somehow managing to retain her expressionless poker face.

Taking a moment to gather herself, JJ finally spoke. "We will need to have copies of all the security videos."

"I'll have them ready within the hour."

JJ nodded stoically. "Also, we'll need a full record of all the hotel staff along with schedules indicating who was on duty before and after the incident took place. And any supporting records we deem necessary."

Montell nodded. "Yes, of course. So you're saying I can count on your help?"

JJ looked at Rebecca and Gwen Q who nodded emphatically. "It's a deal." She held out her hand, and he shook it.

Montell rose to his feet, made a gesture to the barista, and left without a backward glance.

Rebecca turned to JJ with a malevolent smile. "So, what's that you were saying about not being sure?"

CHAPTER 9

Tony Natale winced at the sharp aftertaste of a tequila shot. Normally not a daytime drinker, and never one to touch tequila, he did his best to maintain a party mood and keep up his role as the best man. Logan, the groom-to-be, was standing on the table belting out a Lady Gaga karaoke song in a surprisingly decent voice. The rest of the bachelor's party were on their feet cheering him on.

One of the waitresses approached with a stern-faced look, gesturing for Logan to get down from the table. Logan raised his hands in surrender and clumsily descended from the table, slipping in a patch of water from the half-melted ice bucket as his foot touched the floor. The waitress gasped as Logan's lone standing leg went up in the air. He was going to hit the table hard. Tony moved like lightning from across the room to grab Logan behind the shoulders and ease him to a safe, catastrophe-free landing. Logan looked up at him with a smirk and laughed. "You saved my life, Tony!"

The rest of the groomsmen erupted in cheer. Rabbit, nicknamed for his tendency to jump blindly into just about anything, was the most animated. Though he'd been a serious biochemistry student in college, Rabbit had taken a twisted path since then and ended up a hard-partying used car salesman. 'Pre-owned' cars, he called them. He started to bang the table and lead a chant of "Tony! Tony! Tony!"

Tony shook his head and laughed. "I think that's enough for now, boys." Tony pulled Logan to his feet.

The waitress was clearly delighted to see them go, and Tony gave her a significant tip for her trouble.

Logan—Logue the Rogue—was the fourth person in their group of college friends to get married and had always been the wildcard. None of them had married before the age of forty, and in a few days' time, Tony would be the only one still single. Even Rabbit had tied the knot the year before with a vivacious woman who worked in the office at the car dealership. Logan had insisted before he was even engaged that his bachelor party was going to be a Vegas bash that would shame and humble all bachelor parties that had come before it. They had only been in Las Vegas for a couple of hours and it seemed he was certainly living up to his promise. Having already hit three bars, Tony suggested that it was time for a break, or the groom ran a real risk of not making it out of Vegas alive, let alone to his wedding ceremony.

Tony stood by the door, ushering everyone out and silently counting to make sure no one was missing. They bundled into the waiting limousine and pulled out onto the road.

The limo driver glanced at him through the rearview window. "Where to now, sir?"

"To the hotel," Tony said. "The Neapolitan."

The driver gave a small smile of apparent relief and nodded. "Yes, sir."

Logan had been one of the team of architects who had worked on the re-design for the new and improved Neapolitan hotel, and he insisted on it as the bachelor party's venue. As best man, Tony took care of the hotel reservations and couldn't believe his luck when the Neapolitan called to offer him deeply discounted rates and room upgrades just the day before they arrived. Tony had assumed it was due to Logan's connection with the hotel.

The limo pulled up to the entrance of a behemoth of a building with sliding doors fit to admit an elephant. Outside, men in neon vests were working to take down a sign that read *Welcome to the WIPB*.

Of all the hotels they had driven past, the Neapolitan truly looked to be the most impressive.

Logan slapped Tony's shoulder. "Looks even better than I remember."

They stumbled out of the limo and were aided to the reception desk by the faultless professionalism of the porters who appeared accustomed to having inebriated patrons arrive.

The front desk receptionist seemed delighted to see them. "Welcome to the Neapolitan."

"Thank you, I have a booking under the name Natale. Five rooms." Tony looked around the lobby and found it to be rather sedate for such a prominent hotel on the Strip.

"How are you spelling that, sir?" the receptionist asked.

Tony spelled it out as she typed.

"Ah yes, five double rooms for three nights," she said, as she handed him a tablet with a digital pen. "Could you please fill this form out please?"

When finished, he returned the tablet and leaned over the counter toward the receptionist. "We were granted quite a significant discount on the room rates here. May I ask, to what do we owe the good fortune?"

The receptionist blushed and glanced down at her keyboard. "There . . ." She hesitated. "There was a bit of an incident at the hotel this week, sir."

Tony leaned in a bit further. "What sort of incident?"

"I'm not authorized to speak about that right now, but you'll find a press statement on the homepage of our official website. Nothing that should intrude upon your stay. You will love the Neapolitan."

Tony leaned back, not wanting to press. "I'm sure we will. Thank you."

As the waiting porter arranged their luggage on a cart, Tony pulled his phone out and searched for the Neapolitan website. There at the center of the screen were the words *Press Statement on Winona Dakota*.

Winona Dakota? Tony recognized the name of the former celebrity talk host. He read on with a feeling of trepidation.

The Neapolitan is working with the Las Vegas Metropolitan Police Department in its investigation into the troubling incident surrounding the beloved Winona Dakota, who was a cherished member of the Neapolitan family. Our thoughts and prayers remain with the entire Dakota family at this challenging time. We encourage anyone with any information whatsoever about the incident to please come forward and speak to one of the willing members of the Las Vegas Metropolitan Police Department any time, 24/7, at 1-702-828-7233.

Signed,

The Management and Board of The Neapolitan Hotel and Casino.

Strange. The statement managed to sidestep the nature of this "incident," leaving it unclear whether she was injured, alive, or dead.

He searched for news items on his phone under Winona Dakota's name and clicked on the first headline—*Ex-TV Talk Show Host Suspected Dead in Vegas Robbery.*

The elevator dinged as Tony read. By the time the group arrived at the front door to the first of their five adjoining rooms, Tony had skimmed through three articles on the incident. It appeared that Winona Dakota had been found unconscious in her hotel room with some expensive artwork feared stolen. There was no definitive confirmation that she was dead but every story was clear enough to confirm that her health situation was grave or worse. There were a few blogs carrying sensational, conspiratorial headlines like *Winona Dakota Poisoned in Ritual Killing,* but Tony knew these were likely to be clickbait.

"What is it, Tone?" Rabbit asked as he pushed open the door to his room.

"Yeah," Logan added. "You look like you've seen a ghost."

Tony shook his head, not willing to ruin the start of Logan's bash. "It's nothing. You guys just get some rest. We go again tonight."

Logan flashed a grin. "You know it!"

The rest of the groomsmen decided to take naps, but Tony, clearly the only one who'd been pacing himself, decided to take a walk around the impressive hotel. As he stepped out into the corridor, he passed a trio of suited, stern-faced men who looked as if they were talking business. He flashed a friendly smile, but no one smiled back.

A knot tightened in his stomach. Tony was no stranger to Las Vegas. The last time he had come to the Strip it was to face the same sort of hard-faced men who had been trying to blackmail his father and take down his real estate development company in some underhand deal. Then there was his uncle who'd left Jim Thorpe for Vegas and descended into a life of crime and excess. For all the parties and glitz, Tony knew first-hand the dark underbelly of Sin City. Little went on in Vegas without the watchful eye of the mob. Crime and greed were part of the fabric of Las Vegas, and the crime bosses knew the workings of the city better than anyone. Whatever had transpired with Winona Dakota, he felt sure there was some unsavory connection lurking nearby.

He stepped into the elevator and saw that the number seven for the seventh floor had been papered over with a white sticker that had the word CLOSED written in block capitals. That must have been where the incident happened. He doubted most hotels could afford to close a whole floor for very long. The police were likely just beginning their investigation.

His stomach growled, and he glanced down at his watch. With all the party hoopla upon arrival in Vegas, he just now realized he'd barely eaten since they left Pennsylvania, and it was near dinner time. The diagram in the elevator showed a restaurant on the second floor called *Souk Azou*. He pushed the button for the second floor, exited into the posh corridor, and followed the signs until spotting a Moroccan-style façade with a man wearing a fez at the door.

He stopped to glance at the menu posted outside and nodded to the man his satisfaction.

"Table for one?" asked the man in the fez.

Tony nodded. "Yes, please."

"Right this way, sir," the man said, gesturing inside.

The aroma of mint leaves and mild cardamom filled his nostrils as he entered. The low thrum of Moroccan music and the amber and red-colored glow gave the room an authentic feel. There were few diners, as it was between the lunch and dinner crowds.

"Tony!" came a voice from behind him.

Tony froze and glanced over his shoulder.

JJ Kamaras was waving at him from a corner booth at the edge of the restaurant. He saw two other familiar faces as well—Gwen Q and Rebecca. He hadn't expected to see anyone from home here, let alone JJ and her friends. She smiled at him and beckoned him over. The man who had ushered him into the restaurant gave an approving smile and moved to hold out a seat for him as he joined their table.

JJ locked eyes with him. She seemed both excited and surprised to see him. "What are *you* doing here?"

"I could ask you the same thing," Tony said, wondering why he felt so uneasy when it wasn't like they normally exchanged information about their constant whereabouts when apart.

JJ smiled playfully. "I asked you first."

There was something about her gaze that made him nervous as he cleared his throat to answer. "I'm here for a bachelor party. One of my oldest friends, Logan, is getting married in a couple days."

"No!" Rebecca laughed. "Logue the Rogue?"

Tony nodded. "Do you know him?"

"Of course." She shook her head and smiled. "Used to be a grade A menace at the Jim Thorpe bars back in the day."

"Oh, well he's still a grade A menace," Tony said with a laugh. "How about you guys? Why are you here?"

They all looked at each other as though silently deciding who would do the explaining.

JJ spoke first. "We were invited here for the unveiling of a sculpture at the hotel's museum, but that . . . didn't happen."

Tony raised an eyebrow. "Why not?"

"Winona Dakota invited us. She was found unconscious in her room two days ago."

Tony leaned forward. "I heard about that. What happened?"

"We don't know for sure," JJ said. "She was alone in her room with the sculpture one minute and then, when I found her, she was unconscious, and the sculpture was gone."

"*You* found her?" Tony asked.

She swallowed. "Yes, I did."

"That must have been . . . freaky."

"Yeah." JJ's face appeared to be reliving the incident.

Tony tried to shift the subject. "When are you headed back to Jim Thorpe?"

"Unclear at the moment," JJ answered. "As soon as we find out what happened."

Tony's eyebrows shot up. "Are you . . ."

JJ nodded. "One of the hotel managers has hired us to find out what happened. He wants us to find the sculpture and return it. Says it's worth a fortune, and we three are some of the few who have seen it first hand and know what it looks like. Plus . . ."

Tony leaned forward to hear the rest. "Plus?"

"I may be in a bit of a . . . situation . . . being the last one to see her before the . . . incident."

"Oh." He gave a slow nod. "Well, I have full faith in you. All three of you. If Winona's alive, you'll find her. And the statue."

When it came to solving crime puzzles, JJ Kamaras had a gift. Right up there with his Aunt Constanza. How JJ had managed to solve the murder of his cousin Vito in Italy was beyond him. Her mind simply worked in special ways, seeing details and patterns where others couldn't. She didn't stop until she uncovered the truth—the true spirit of a detective, Constanza would say.

"Thank you," Rebecca said with a smile, as Gwen nodded along.

The four of them sat quietly for a moment until a loud ping broke the silence. JJ looked down at the notification on her phone. Her expression shifted from one of dogged determination to one of despair.

"What is it?" Rebecca asked.

JJ held up her phone, displaying the message. "It's Winona. She has just been confirmed dead."

The news sent a ripple of emotion through the table. Gwen Q, whom Tony had never seen look even remotely upset, appeared deeply distraught, and Rebecca's cheerful smile melted away into a pained, sour-faced frown.

"So this is a murder investigation now," JJ said stoically.

"Our fourth," Rebecca added.

"We're three for three," Gwen explained to Tony, raising her chin resolutely. "And we'll be four for four. We'll find who is responsible and bring them in. We have to."

Tony nodded and drew in a heavy breath. "How can I help?"

Just then a voice broke in from behind them.

"There he is!"

It was Logan's voice, loud and unmistakable. Tony turned toward his old friend, praying that he had recovered from their afternoon indulgence.

Logan was dressed smartly and walked with the corporate poise that Tony had seen him display when the occasion called for it. *And he's only half sober.*

He extended a hand to each of the women, shaking them one after another and introducing himself with his ultra-charming smile. "I'm Logan Sonnen."

"The man of the hour," Tony added.

Logan grinned and glanced up at the ceiling. Never one for humility, he continued. "You know, I was actually one of the architects who designed this building."

"Really?" JJ seemed genuinely impressed.

"Yup." He nodded proudly. "Back when I was single and wild and fun."

"Ah, yes," Rebecca quipped.

Their booth was only meant for a party of four, so Tony rose to his feet. "We're going to find our own table. It was a real pleasure seeing you ladies." He turned to JJ and mouthed the words *call me*.

She gave a nod of understanding.

Tony walked away and admittedly felt relieved. JJ didn't seem bothered that he was in Sin City for a bachelor party with Jim Thorpe's most notorious ladies' man. He initially felt compelled to give the

"It's not what it looks like" speech, but when JJ seemed undaunted, he decided against it. He could be trusted, and hopefully, she knew it.

Still, an unsettling sensation lingered for Tony. Whether it was his just past associations with Vegas, or the news of Winona's death, the faintly foreboding feeling persisted.

Shake it off, Tone, and put on your party face.

CHAPTER 10

The front entrance of the Neapolitan was nearly barricaded with a wall of press and media personnel. The death of Winona Dakota had dominated the news cycle for the four hours since it was aired.

The World International Poker Bowl was canceled, and the Neapolitan had transformed from a hub of frenetic activity to a dour space of quiet reflection.

JJ, Gwen, and Rebecca were assembled in a small meeting room that Montell had arranged as their base. At JJ's invitation and with Montell's permission, Tony also joined them. A panel of screens, organized per Rebecca's design, was set against the longest wall, while a whiteboard with multi-colored markers was placed on the adjoining one. JJ strode up to the board and wrote the word *Arapaho* at its center.

"Our primary task," she began, "is to find the Arapaho."

Gwen Q gave an affirming nod.

JJ wrote the name Winona Dakota on another corner of the board. "We also have to find out exactly what happened to Winona. I know it isn't what Montell is paying us to do, but it's just as important, if not more so, than finding the Arapaho."

"Got it. Where do we start?" Tony asked.

"With the security footage," JJ said, nodding to Rebecca.

Rebecca clicked the remote control, and the screens came alive with grayscale security footage.

"That camera shows the corridor outside Winona's room," Rebecca said, pointing. "That one shows the elevator area, and that one is right above the emergency exit."

They watched carefully as the footage began to play.

"There she is," Rebecca said, as Winona Dakota appeared on the screen. The time at the bottom of the screen was 2:17 p.m. Winona must have just been coming from the museum.

The screen went blank for a second, and then the footage returned.

"What was that?" Tony asked.

"A connection error," Rebecca explained. "Not uncommon with large-scale surveillance systems like this one. Signal gets weak or a camera fails or a power surge causes a break in transmission. It's why you need multiple cameras to ensure you always have a view of what's going on."

The footage continued as Winona reached her room and slid her keycard in to open her door. She must have heard something because she paused with the door open and glanced back into the corridor. A uniformed man with a tool bag came into view, and they entered Winona's room together. He exited at 2:31 p.m. and closed the door. Then at 2:35 a matronly woman pushing a cleaning cart passed by and continued down the hall. The footage continued with hardly any movement for several minutes. More than once, there were connection errors which rendered the screen blank on one camera or the other for a second or two each time. Then, at 2:45 p.m., a figure appeared from the emergency stairwell. He wore a beige baseball cap which he kept pulled low and walked with his face half turned away from the camera. He looked to be a man under age forty, and JJ was almost certain that he was the man with the handlebar mustache. He was dressed like a janitor and had a bag with him—one easily big enough to steal the Arapaho.

The strange man knocked on Winona's door and after a few seconds, she answered. They spoke briefly in the corridor before she let him inside. At 2:50 p.m., he emerged on the screen again, with Winona visible inside her room waving goodbye to him, but the video was very choppy.

JJ narrowed her eyes. *She was alive when he left.* Or at least alive enough to walk to the door.

More time passed and more connection errors were visible. At 2:52 p.m., JJ appeared on screen. Now Winona's door was ajar, and JJ knocked and went inside. They continued to play the footage for the next few minutes until the emergency services workers had left with Winona's body. Then Rebecca stopped it.

JJ put her hand to her forehead, blown away by the knowledge they had just watched Winona Dakota's last moments. Winona looked utterly unaware that death was imminent. She was taken by complete surprise.

Tony shifted in his seat and made a low sound in his throat.

"Thoughts anyone?" Rebecca asked at last.

JJ furrowed her brow. "So two men went in and out before I arrived. Opportunities to steal the Arapaho and perhaps set something in motion to kill Winona. The second one with the handlebar mustache looks guiltier to me. Plus, he barged right into me near the elevator and was in a rush to leave. But with the video so erratic, it's hard to see if he left with anything."

"If you have a gut feeling on him, maybe he's our man," Tony said.

JJ leaned forward with a pensive look. "Why would he be so careless?"

"Maybe he isn't very clever," Rebecca offered. "He was probably hired to just snatch the sculpture and split. Not every crime is the work of a mastermind. Though he did seem to know enough to avoid looking directly into any of the cameras and kept his head low."

Rebecca made sense. It looked like a simple enough case of a man tricking his way into the hotel room and grabbing the sculpture he had arrived to steal. But JJ couldn't shake the feeling that there was more than what met the eye. Something they were missing.

Gwen Q touched JJ's shoulder. "We shouldn't overthink it—maybe it really is this simple."

"Maybe," JJ said, trailing off. "Next question: how did he kill her?"

"The coroner's report will tell us that soon enough," Rebecca said. "Maybe he struck her."

JJ shook her head, unconvinced. "No, I don't think so. There was no blood." She hesitated. "And besides, she wouldn't wave goodbye to someone who just attacked her."

"What if he used some sort of chemical or poison?" Gwen suggested.

JJ shrugged and looked deep in thought.

"What else do you think could have happened?" Tony asked gently.

JJ tapped on the table. "I . . . I'm not sure."

"Well, JJ, if you don't think it is those men, given the footage we just saw . . ." Rebecca hesitated. "Then the only other person that could be responsible . . ."

They all looked at Rebecca expectantly, waiting for her to continue.

"Is you."

JJ's eyes widened. How had she not even considered it would look that way? Especially after Officer Tyrell's accusing tone—that alone was enough to know the Las Vegas police were no friends of hers. If they found any reason to suspect JJ, they would take it. If it wasn't the men in the video, she was suspect number one. *It has to be the handlebar mustache guy.*

"You're all right," JJ said at last. "That has to be our man."

"Thank you." Rebecca let out a relieved breath. "So how do we find him?"

JJ was about to answer when Tony's phone buzzed. He glanced down at the screen and declined the call. "Sorry about that," he said, raising a hand in apology.

JJ nodded. "Where were we?"

"I was asking how we find the man with the handlebar mustache."

"Right," JJ said. "We start with the staff list. See who was on duty that day and if anyone recognizes him. Also, we've arranged a meeting to talk with some members of the Dakota family out in Reno. They might have some useful information for us on how Winona managed to get the Arapaho sculpture."

Tony's phone buzzed again, and he looked exasperated.

"It's okay. You should take it," JJ urged.

He gave an apologetic look and then answered. "Hey Logan, I'm—"

Whatever Logan had said made him stop short. You could hear the echo of Logan's frantic voice as he spoke. The color seemed to drain from Tony's face as he listened.

"Where are you?" Tony asked.

Logan droned out an answer.

"I'm coming now."

JJ's eyes widened. "What is it?"

But Tony was already running through the door.

* * *

Tony burst into the waiting room of the intensive care unit. His shirt was sticky with sweat and his heart was still thumping. He had run at a dead sprint all the way from the parking lot.

"How can I help you, sir?" a nurse asked.

He tried to gather his breath to answer then spotted Logan seated to the right of her. "Logan."

His friend turned to him and rose to his feet. Tony stepped close and saw from Logan's pink-red eyes that the man had either been drinking heavily, crying profusely, or both.

"It's Rabbit," Logan said, "I don't know what he took, but he's having a really bad reaction. They're saying he may have had a stroke."

Tony narrowed his eyes. "What do you mean, what he took?"

Logan lowered his chin. "We were getting some stuff for tonight. Planning on having a really good time, that's all. Rabbit bought some special whiskey from some dude. Spiked with some stuff, I'm sure. Said he just wanted to make sure it was primo before tonight."

Tony frowned. It was no coincidence his friends had decided to pull a stunt like this while they knew he would be away. He would never have gone along with it.

"Who sold it to you?" Tony asked.

Logan looked at the floor. "He's Rabbit's friend, not mine. I only just met him."

Tony spoke slowly, with increasing volume. *"Who sold it to you?"*

"Some guy named Tim." Logan closed his eyes and tilted his head back. "Rabbit knows him from back home. Promised to show us a good time out here. Rabbit admitted he's into some shady stuff."

"Tim who?"

"I think the last name's Ream."

The name struck a chord with Tony. He'd heard it from JJ before. *Tim Ream.*

A nurse appeared behind Logan and tapped his shoulder to get his attention. "You can go in to see him now."

Tony and Logan followed her into the hospital room. Rabbit lay in a metal bed with white linens and an IV drip connected to his forearm. He looked like he'd been run over by a truck from the inside out. His face was drained of color, and his eyes were barely open. He tried a smile but the tremor in his cheek made it uncomfortable to watch.

Rabbit glanced up at Tony. "Don't worry, Tone. I know. It was stupid. No more."

Tony didn't say a word. This was a narrow escape, and Tony was going to find the man responsible.

Tim Ream.

CHAPTER 11

*R*eno was, in some strange way, a parody of Las Vegas. As they drove down North Virginia Street, JJ thought it was like a novice painter had tried to recreate the Strip but couldn't quite get the colors right to match the original. The casinos were smaller, and the hotels were not quite as tall. Compared to the glamour and pulsating chaos of Vegas, people out on the Reno strip seemed to carry on nonchalantly, as if they had nine-to-fives waiting for them in the morning.

The Dakota family home was within throwing distance of a giant Costco outlet store at the corner of the University of Nevada campus. It had the sunken, lived-in feel of a house that had been passed from generation to generation.

Noah pulled their vehicle up on the corner of the driveway, knowing it was too big to go any further. His distaste was visible when he noticed the side of the Lincoln Navigator was tracked with dirt from riding down the sand-dusted Nevada roads.

"I'll be waiting right here, ladies," he said as they climbed down from the car.

"Thanks, Noah," Rebecca said.

They walked up to the door and pressed the doorbell. The soft infrared light of a camera preceded the sound of footsteps behind the door.

The door opened to reveal a young man who looked to be in his late twenties. His eyes widened at their arrival, and he thrust his hand out for a handshake.

"You're JJ Kamaras," he said, with a note of excitement.

JJ nodded and shook his hand. "Pleased to meet you."

He turned to Rebecca. "And you must be Rebecca Brannigan."

Rebecca seemed surprised at this recognition, as the fame from their earlier exploits generally had been ascribed to JJ.

The young man turned last of all to Gwen Q and grinned.

Gwen extended her hand. "I'm—"

"Gwen Quinones," he finished. "Beautiful master of disguise."

Gwen Q stood back and smiled. "Wow."

His grin widened. "I'm Cody Dakota. Winona's nephew. I've read all about you guys. I run the blog *World's Greatest True Detectives*. You may have heard of it."

It was obvious by the trio's expressions that no one had, but they gave encouraging smiles just the same.

"A pleasure to meet you Cody," JJ said.

He shook his head, ushering them inside. "No, the pleasure is all mine. I am a big fan of your work. All of you. I followed the Vito Natale case like a hawk. I was like *what?* when they said it was that sous chef. How did you figure that one out?"

He was looking at Rebecca.

"Serious investigation tactics." Rebecca shrugged. "A bit of luck."

"Interesting!" Cody grinned. "Please come in."

They strode into the house and found that the living room had that same, lived-in feel that the exterior had. The home clearly hadn't seen a paint job or new décor since roller disco.

Cody gestured toward the cracked leather sofa dotted with fuzzy throw pillows.

"We are so sorry for your loss, Cody," JJ began. "Winona was lovely, and we only knew her so briefly. We can't imagine what your family is going through right now."

"Thank you," he said with a faint smile. "Winona was the sweetest of all my aunts. I'll really miss her."

JJ nodded. "She was very kind to us, too."

"I told her about you," Cody said. "Sent her all your stories. Then she called me to tell me she was thinking of inviting you to Las Vegas to unveil the family sculpture."

JJ face showed her intrigue. "The *family* sculpture?"

He shot back a confused look. "Oh, man. You don't know, do you?"

"Know what?" Rebecca asked.

"Our family has Native American roots, from the Arapaho tribe. That sculpture had been in the care of our family for generations. It was lost in a fire by one of our great grandfathers and only found again recently. Winona was insistent about finding the right home for it. She thought it was too precious to have it here. Plus, some of my uncles were pressuring her to sell it, so she probably wanted to keep it away from them."

JJ gave a nod and brought out her notebook, jotting down what Cody had said so far.

"So, we need to ask," JJ began, "if you know anyone who might have wanted to hurt Winona."

Cody shook his head. "No. I don't. Everyone loved her. Even all my nasty uncles. Her talk show ran for years. She always knew how to talk to people and was really diplomatic. Knew how to keep everyone on the same side. I find it hard to believe that anyone I know could want to hurt her."

Though JJ rarely forgot recounted details, she continued to jot down highlights just in case.

"About the sculpture," she began, "who could possibly have wanted to take it?"

"Oh, well that's different." Cody lowered his head. "Anyone who knew about it. Winona's dad had someone take a look at a picture of it before he passed a few years back—some kind of expert—who said it would be worth around ten million dollars if it was legit."

JJ's eyes widened. "Ten million dollars?"

Cody nodded. "That's what I heard. Half the family has wanted to sell it ever since. Winona had to fight hard to get everyone behind this idea of keeping it."

Rebecca leaned forward to ask a question of her own. "You said it was lost in a fire a while back?"

"That was what we initially thought."

"So how was it found again?" Gwen asked.

"It turned out it was hidden away in a safe, though the house around it was in ashes. Winona and my dad were the ones who managed to decipher the code and recover the sculpture. They are the only ones who saw it."

"I see," JJ said. If what Cody was saying was true, it meant that most of the Dakota members were potential suspects in the incident at The Neapolitan.

"They tried to steal it once," Cody said. "Some thieves got in through the back window and tried to swipe the sculpture, but Dad fended them off, and they didn't get near it. That was when Winona knew that a museum was the best place to keep it."

JJ nodded her understanding and turned to Rebecca who looked as though she had a question of her own to ask.

"Do you live here by yourself, Cody?" Rebecca asked.

His eyes seemed to brighten. "My uncle is in and out. My sister's at college and in and out. Every now and then other members of the family come in town and stay. At the moment, it's just me. But, if you want to talk to anyone else in the family, I'm sure we could arrange it."

Rebecca looked pensive. "I know this might be a tough ask, but I was wondering if you had a family tree or something like that, so we could run checks on the other surviving members of the family?"

"Nah, I don't think we have anything like that. Closest thing we have to something like that is our family portrait," he said, pointing.

JJ glanced over her shoulder and noticed the giant framed photograph just behind them. The moment she saw it, she gasped.

Winona was immediately recognizable at the center of the portrait, as was Cody, but the face that sent a tremor through her was the man with a thick, dark, handlebar mustache. It was uncanny. He looked exactly like the man who had run into her at the elevator in the Neapolitan, just a little older.

"When was this taken?" JJ asked, walking up to stare closely at the photograph.

Cody shrugged. "About fifteen years ago. Maybe even longer. I was just a kid then," he said pointing at a smiling, younger iteration of Cody.

JJ raised a hand to point at the man with the handlebar mustache. "Who is this?"

"That is my Uncle Jacobi. He's on my dad's side."

"Does he live in Nevada?" JJ asked.

Cody shook his head. "Uncle Jacobi died a long time ago. At least ten years now."

JJ leaned toward him. "You're sure?"

Cody nodded. "Positive. He was buried here in Reno. Lawton John Cemetery. Same place as my dad."

JJ made a hurried note as he spoke.

Cody started to point out other people in the photograph. "These are uncles and cousins over here. And here . . ."

JJ listened absently as she tried to make sense of what Cody had just told her about the man with the handlebar mustache. *Uncle Jacobi died a long time ago.*

She had only seen him a split second, but he looked so similar to the face of the man she had bumped into outside the elevator. *Maybe he's not dead. Then again, the one at the hotel looked younger. Ugh, that makes no sense.*

When they had no more questions to ask, Cody offered them every beverage and snack imaginable to get them to stay a while longer. The longer they were in his company, the more they realized his interest in their detective exploits was very real. He rattled off details of their previous investigations down to the names of the police officers involved.

Before they left, he insisted on giving each of them his cell phone number, email address, password to access exclusive posts on his blog, and finally his Instagram handle—@truecrimecody. They accepted it all with appreciation and left to rejoin Noah in the Lincoln.

JJ insisted they visit the Lawton John cemetery to confirm that Jacobi Dakota was indeed dead and buried. It was a small cemetery, but it still took them a good half hour to find his resting place. Yet there it was. According to the headstone, the man had died ten years prior, just as Cody had said.

The drive back to Vegas was a deeply contemplative one as JJ started to wonder if she'd been correct about the resemblance between the man she had seen at the Neapolitan and the one in the family photograph.

She browsed memorial websites and found pictures of Jacobi Dakota on a forevermissed.com page that corresponded to the family photograph. Apparently, it *was* him and he *was* dead.

"We need to look deeper into the family," Rebecca said. "See if there's anyone in the family who looks like Jacobi."

JJ agreed. "At least we have a name."

"True." Rebecca let out a heavy breath. "Have you heard from Tony yet?"

JJ nodded. "His friend gets out of the ICU today. Apparently, that whiskey was mixed with Everclear—190 proof—and spiked with amphetamines and ecstasy. He's really lucky he's alive."

"Wow," Gwen Q said. "Nasty stuff."

"Right. Plus, there was something else he told me when we spoke," JJ added with a hint of trepidation.

Rebecca quirked up an eyebrow. "What?"

"The guy who sold his friend the spiked booze was none other than our good friend Tim Ream."

"Well, what do you know? You mean the same Tim Ream who swore up and down he was on the straight and narrow last time we saw him?" Rebecca shook her head.

"Same one," JJ said. "Of course, he was never exactly the trustworthy type, so how surprised can we be?"

The more JJ thought of it, the more uncomfortable she felt about the fact that Tim Ream, Johnny Golden, and Bruce Balvin had all converged on Vegas the same week she was there *and* a priceless statue was scheduled to be displayed. Even with the World International Poker Bowl as a backdrop, seeing these treacherous faces from the past under the same roof at the same time made her very uneasy.

"Speak of the devil and he shall appear," Gwen Q said, pointing out the vehicle window.

JJ glanced up and saw none other than Tim Ream standing beside a designer golf bag and dressed like he was just about to tee off.

"That's him," JJ said.

Noah pulled over behind a row of cars, and JJ hopped out. Just as she closed in on him, she noticed Tony Natale coming from the other direction, his eyes also fixed on Tim Ream. JJ quickened her step, unsure what Tony planned to do to him and desperate to get her question in first.

"Tim," she called out. "Tim Ream."

The man turned slowly toward her, and a devious grin grew on his face. "Well, if it isn't Jim Thorpe's dollar store Sherlock Holmes."

How JJ wished Rebecca had been there to deliver a razor-quick retort. When it came to Sherlockian quips, Rebecca had no equal.

"What are you doing here, Tim?" JJ said, her voice rising over the grumble of car engines.

"It's a free country, last time I checked."

"Not for much longer," came another voice.

Tony stood behind Tim Ream and looked at him with daggers in his eyes.

Tim Ream looked at JJ, then back at Tony. "What's going on here?"

Tony lifted Tim Ream's golf bag. "Why don't we sit and talk in the hotel lobby," Tony said calmly. "The weather isn't good for golf anyway."

Tim Ream gave Tony a menacing look, but something in Tony's tone and the set of his jaw must have made him relent. "All right then, let's talk."

CHAPTER 12

The hotel lobby was blissfully quiet. Tim Ream ordered a whisky and coke, and JJ opted for freshly squeezed orange juice. Tony made no order. The entire time, his eyes were locked tight on Tim Ream. Gwen Q and Rebecca had left to do some internet research into the Dakota family tree, particularly the deceased man with the handlebar mustache.

Tim had his arms crossed in front of him as he sat opposite JJ and Tony. "So, what do you want to know?"

Tony opened his mouth to speak, but JJ beat him to the punch. "Why are you here?"

Tim glared at JJ, took a long sip of whiskey, and set his glass down methodically. "I came here for the poker tournament. Nothing else. Johnny Golden and I have been talking about coming to the WIPB for years. Not here for no trouble. I told you before, I'm clean now."

"Clean enough to be selling bad drugs?" Tony hissed.

"I don't sell drugs."

Tony leaned forward and spoke low. "Oh, yes, you do."

A short silence passed, and the tension was thick as a wall between the two men. Tony seemed to fight to retain his calm.

"All right," Tim Ream said, raising his hands. "A few extra hits in the whiskey. Guy kept saying he wanted to have a good time! College girls do heavier stuff than that." He shot JJ an ugly smirk. "Though I was a bit insulted they assumed I was a drug dealer. I mean, I'm an upstanding citizen."

Tony leaned toward him and snarled.

"Look, I didn't have any pills on me, so I scored a few on the Strip and gave the bachelor party guy what he wanted. He practically begged me, man! So, I made $300 off the top. Pocket change. No idea where the stuff came from."

"I don't believe you," Tony said.

Tim Ream shrugged. "Suit yourself, but it's the absolute truth. Got no drugs with me. Not a drug dealer. I just scammed some guys that were begging to be scammed."

"You almost killed my friend."

"Your friend? Tim laughed. "That's what this is about? Big deal, some out-of-town dude comes to party and gets some bad Vegas drugs. That's like a rite of passage out here. Loosen up, bro! Believe me, if I hadn't gotten them the stuff, someone else would have."

Tony kept his gaze fixed on Tim. "Where'd you get the drugs, Ream?"

After a long silence, Tim gave in. "Fine. I got the junk from a dude named Ted Cookie. They call him the Cookie Monster. He's a street-level dealer but has connections all the way up to the richest of the rich. Been in the game for a long time. Also the best pick-pocketer in the Western Hemisphere."

"Such an honor." JJ rolled her eyes.

Tony's frown deepened and he remained solely focused on Tim's face.

JJ knew that he had committed the name to memory, just as she had. "What about Bruce Balvin? What is he doing here?"

"That's way, *way* above my pay grade, chica."

"I'm sure you have some ideas."

"Bruce Balvin is deep in the gambling world. You know that. No surprise he'd be in Las Vegas for an international poker tournament. He comes to the old casino in Jim Thorpe, and it's kiddie stuff for him. But here in Vegas, it's the big leagues. He's got deep connections here—loan-sharking, illegal betting, drugs. Bruce Balvin's got his hands in all of it."

JJ blinked. "Meaning he might be involved with the incident at the Neapolitan?"

"I'd say it's a safe bet. *If* I were a gambling man, that is." Tim threw his head back and laughed.

Tony did not look amused.

JJ stared at Tim squarely. "How do I know you're not just trying to shift the focus away from yourself?"

His guttural laugh deepened, the table trembling gently as he spoke. "You can focus on me all you want, little girl, but you'll be wasting your time. I don't get involved in snooty art heists. Thanks to you and that bust up at the casino, I left even the small stuff behind. I can't be that guy anymore."

There was something in Tim Ream's voice that caught her off-guard. He almost sounded believable.

She cleared her throat. "Where do I find Bruce Balvin?"

He grinned. "Oh, information like that is going to cost you." He held his empty glass up to a waiter. "I presume drinks are on you?"

JJ gave a reluctant nod.

"Then $100 to hear where Bruce Balvin will be tonight."

JJ let out a resigned breath. "Fine."

Tim Ream accepted his now-refilled glass of whiskey and smiled. "There's a bar called the Monza. It's off the Strip, down one of the side streets. All the big fish in Vegas go there every Thursday. It's like a meet and greet for all the baddest gangsters in the city. Bruce Balvin is gonna be there. I'm sure of it."

JJ slid a $100 bill silently across the table. "How do we get into the Monza bar?"

Tim Ream shrugged. "That I can't tell you. It's heavyweights only. They don't let people like me in that place. Let's just say, they're the kind of criminals who *don't* get mistaken for drug dealers in five-dollar karaoke bars. They rub shoulders with politicians and movie stars. From what I hear, you need a secret phone number from one of the members, then text for a password."

Tony slid his cell phone out of his pocket and typed into the Google search bar.

"You won't find it." Tim grinned lasciviously as he stuffed the bill in his pocket.

JJ sat back in her chair. "I'm guessing you don't have the secret phone number."

"If I did, you'd be paying me a lot more money right now."

JJ rose to her feet. "A real pleasure doing business with you, Tim."

He gave a mocking bow and grinned. "Oh, the pleasure's all mine, Pan Am."

JJ glared at him. She hated it when he brought up her old nickname as if they were close friends.

"Her name's Julia." Tony stayed rooted to his seat without moving. "And this dealer you mentioned, Ted Cookie. What's he look like?"

Ream shot the rest of his drink and coughed. "Skinny white guy with red dreadlocks to the waist. Wears a big gold chain with a golden cookie on the pendant. You can find him at a bar called the Star. He's there every night. He ain't hard to find."

Tony gave a solemn nod and rose to his feet. "If I find out even one thing you told us is a lie, I'll do everything I can to make sure you spend the rest of your days in a dark cell."

Ream let out a howl of a laugh. "Yeah, whatever."

They had both turned to leave when Tim called out to them. "This isn't Jim Thorpe, baby Sherlock. Stay far away from this one. Just drink your little Shirley Temples and go back home to Pennsylvania. This goes way beyond anything you can handle."

JJ faced him, her stare steady. "You have no idea what I can handle."

Something in her eyes must have sold it because big and burly Tim Ream became silent and walked away.

Tony and JJ left the bar and walked side by side in silence until they arrived at the elevator.

"I'm sorry about what happened to your friend," JJ said.

Tony shook his head. "Ream wasn't lying about that part. Logan told me everything. They *were* looking to take the party up a notch—though I doubt they knew exactly what they were getting themselves into. Still, totally stupid and reckless. They're not teenagers."

"Just glad he's okay."

Tony gave a crumpled smile. "Right, it could have been way worse. Rabbit could have died. How his wife puts up with him, I'll never understand."

A ping sounded as the elevator arrived.

"I'll catch up with you later," Tony said.

"Where are you going?"

Tony met JJ's gaze. "To find Ted Cookie."

JJ took a breath in, as if to say something, then stopped. She looked at him with concern in her eyes. "Even if you find him, what are you going to do? Call the police on him?"

Tony hesitated. It was a good question. "I just want to check Tim Ream's story out. If this Ted Cookie guy's really been selling drugs in Vegas this long, I bet he knows a thing or two about the Monza Club. I Googled it while he was talking, and he was right—nothing. Wherever it is, it's a secret, and even if we find it, there's no way we get in without that password. I have a feeling that Ted Cookie might be the key to getting us in there."

JJ straightened. "I'll come with you."

Tony shook his head. "I'm going alone on this one, JJ. The Star sounds like a bad place. I'll text you as soon as I know something."

JJ glanced up at him and gave a nod of understanding. "All right then. How about we meet later tonight by the museum café?"

Tony nodded. "Deal."

CHAPTER 13

Tony left the hotel and set out to navigate his way to the Star. It was just past four in the afternoon when he finally found the place. It was an old, dusty building with a sign illuminated by a flickering fluorescent light and it was desperately in need of renovations. He gritted his teeth and nudged the door open.

Deafening rap music was blaring from mounted speakers at the four corners of the room. The lighting was dim, making it difficult to see the faces of the people seated in both the booths and at the bar.

Tony could feel the attention on him as he strode toward the bar. Clearly, this was the sort of place where all the patrons were regulars and outsiders never darkened the door. Half a glance was all it took to know the beer was bad and the bathrooms were worse. The Star was in direct contrast to the glitz and glamour of the Strip—it was a dirty, low-down locals' bar. Tony stuck out like a sore thumb.

Steeling himself, he stepped up to the bar and tapped the counter to get some attention—a rude gesture, but Tony considered it fitting for the Star. A male and female duo behind the bar glanced over at him and then at each other in silent negotiation before the young woman decided to answer his call.

What Tony really felt like drinking was an espresso, but he looked weird enough.

"I'll take a draft beer," he said.

The bartender, perhaps sensing the rare opportunity for a generous tip, flashed a wide smile and nodded. "Coming right up."

Tony tapped his foot impatiently as he cast a covert glance about the bar. There was no sign of Ted Cookie. With the lighting so dim, even a white man with red dreads to his waist might be hard to discern here. Add the booming music, and any attempt to overhear conversations was nearly useless as well.

"Here you are" The bartender pushed a beer mug across the counter.

Tony gave her an appreciative smile and sipped slowly, working out a plan in his mind. He had to find a way to use the prying eyes around the bar, all glued to him at the moment, to his advantage.

Finishing his drink, he slid over a twenty-dollar bill to the bartender. She grinned appreciatively and turned back to the register. Tony headed for the closest booth. *This may just work.*

As he sauntered past each booth, faces came into the dull glow of light and he inspected each in turn. None of them matched the description that Tim Ream had given. No skinny guys with red dreadlocks. All the same, Tony squeezed in the edge of a full booth.

"Anyone looking for more than beer?" he asked, with the hint of a smile.

The closest man to him, a bearded man with legs like ham hocks, gave him a disgusted look and turned away. Another looked almost afraid and insisted he wanted no part of what Tony was offering.

One man waved Tony on. "No way. Get lost."

Unperturbed, Tony proceeded to the next table and repeated the question. The patrons at the second booth were even less receptive to his solicitation with one of them waving his arm angrily. He was not making any friends here.

A hand fell upon his shoulder just before he reached the third booth. A low, threatening voice rumbled behind him. "What do you think you're doing, slick?"

Jackpot.

Tony suppressed a smile as he turned slowly. Standing behind him, with arms folded across his thin chest was a man with red dreadlocks that fell to the waist and a thick gold chain with a golden cookie pendant. He had giant earrings in each lobe and had a slight slouch that made him seem smaller than he actually was.

"Nothing," Tony said, snatching his shoulder away.

Ted Cookie glared without blinking and emphasized each word he spoke. *"Do you even know where you are?"*

Ted Cookie's face of scars and old bruises told his story. He snarled at Tony, and the gleaming jewels in his teeth and the tattoo of a devil winding up his neck added to his menacing image.

Tony was undeterred. "Let's talk this over outside."

Ted Cookie hesitated and squinted in Tony's direction. Tony knew, in that moment, the man was weighing his options. Tony had taken a hefty gamble—but hey, it was Vegas, after all.

"Outside, then," he hissed.

Tony gestured toward the door, making sure to keep his distance as they stepped out of the bar.

Ted Cookie leaned against the shabby outside wall as his gold chain glistened in the setting sun. His left hand seemed to be nearly imperceptibly making its way to his waistband, just above a bulging pocket, which Tony felt sure contained a pistol.

Tony drew in a deep breath and let it out slowly. "I'm no dealer."

Ted looked him up and down. "Well, that's obvious."

Tony nodded. "I came here looking for you, in particular."

Ted tucked his hand in his waistband again and fixed Tony with a suspicious glare. "Really."

Tony's heart was thumping in his chest but he managed to retain an outward calm. "A friend of mine told me about you. Said you ran things down here and knew everything there is to know about Vegas. Where I'm from, when you come to a new kingdom, you first pay homage to the king."

Ted crossed his arms and stared squarely at Tony for a long moment. His suspicion appeared to fade ever so slightly and a faint smile started to appear. "I've been out here near fifteen years. Yeah, I know a thing or two."

Tony gave a smile. "I knew you were the man to see."

Ted tapped his chain. "See for what?"

"There's this club I heard about. Really exclusive. They said that you run things down there. I'd do anything to take my girl there tonight, just once. Anything."

Ted raised an eyebrow. "I don't know what club you're talking about."

Tony tried to sound casual. "The Monza."

Ted's eyes widened for a moment, then narrowed with renewed suspicion. "What do you know about the Monza?"

"I know you're the only man in Las Vegas who has the power to get me in there."

It was a flat-out lie, as there were likely others with connections who could get them in. Still, flattery seemed to have been working thus far, so Tony thought he'd keep dishing it out. He could almost see the cogs in Ted Cookie's mind turning. He was beginning to bite.

"It'll cost you."

Tony nodded, scarcely able to believe his luck. "How much exactly?"

Ted stared at the sky as though counting numbers. "Two hundred bucks."

Tony took a moment to feign weighing the offer. "Two hundred dollars. Okay."

"I can get you in tonight but you have to play it cool when you get there."

"Me and my girl?"

"Fine." He pointed at Tony and leaned toward him. "Don't make a scene."

"Right." Tony handed him a pen from his shirt pocket.

Ted took the pen, pulled a business card from his pocket, and wrote on it. "133 Eastern Boulevard. Right by Fremont Street." Then, he wrote a phone number below it and handed the card to Tony. "Text this number for a password. At the door, say you're with the Cookie Monster."

Tony grinned and extended a hand. "Thanks, man."

Ted glanced down at the hand and frowned. "Now get out of my sight."

Tony turned and started to walk away when Ted let out a wicked laugh. He spun around to face Ted.

"Missing something, GQ?" He shook his head and smirked as he dangled Tony's gold watch. "Don't be such a doofus. You'll embarrass me." He tossed the watch to Tony, who caught it with one hand.

Tony pressed his lips together and clenched his jaw as he fought to restrain himself. He'd gotten what he came for—info about the Monza. He shot Ted a long, steely glare, then turned and walked away.

CHAPTER 14

*R*ebecca's phone vibrated in her pocket. The name on the screen sent a cold shiver of dread through her. Her ex-husband John only ever called when he had trouble to start.

"Excuse me," she said to Gwen and JJ as she stepped out from the museum café to take the call.

Once alone, she closed her eyes and whispered to herself, "Do not let him get to you." Steadying herself, she answered.

John sounded irritated when he replied. "Well, hello, party girl. Having a good time?"

Rebecca could hear the unmistakable voices in the background from Sesame Street. A surefire sign that her daughter was close by watching television. That made her smile—hopefully, Abi was doing okay.

"Yes. How are you?"

John scoffed. "Oh, I'm just dandy."

Rebecca drew in another breath, bracing herself for whatever it was John had coming next. *Don't let him get to you.*

"So," he began. "What's the name of your hotel out there in Las Vegas?"

Rebecca hesitated. "Why?"

"Why?" John's voice thickened with sarcasm and irritation. "Only because I'm being a responsible parent, Rebecca. I need to know where you are. We have a child together, remember? Plus, I was watching the news the other day and heard about this fatal armed robbery in Las Vegas and worried it was at your hotel."

In times gone by, Rebecca might have been fooled by this slick maneuver of faux concern but she knew John so much better than that now. Concern was always his Trojan horse for control, and she wasn't opening the gates anymore. *Don't let him get to you.*

"I'm safe and sound," Rebecca said. "Don't you worry about that. My mom in Pittsburgh has all my information, in the unlikely event it's ever needed. Obviously, you can just call me on my cell if you need—if Abi needs me."

His façade of patience faded, and he raised his voice. "What are you hiding?"

"Nothing."

"You're doing that stupid detective thing again, aren't you? You and your friends are up to your teenage shenanigans."

"So, how's Abi?"

"Oh, so you remember you have a daughter! You can't just run off whenever you feel like it to go play Nancy Drew, you know."

Rebecca felt her resolve stretch to the point of breaking, and it took an almighty effort to avoid taking the bait and firing back. "Can I just talk to Abi, please?"

"No," John snarled. "You don't get to just waltz in and out with her when you please."

Rebecca felt something within snap at that. The absolute gall of this man who'd left them when Abi was a baby and had the nerve to project *his* waltzing in and out on her.

"Are you bloody kidding me?" she asked, incredulous. "You leave us and show up four years later and now see our daughter two weekends in a good year and call *me* irresponsible? Look, I told you, my neighbor, Mrs. Henson, could have watched her for the week, no problem. Or I could have taken her to Pittsburgh to my mom's house. I should have known you'd pull something. Tell you what. I'll make you a deal. You tell me her birthday right now, and I'll pack my bags and be on the next flight."

The line went quiet for a long moment. Rebecca shuddered that she'd let John get under her skin like this. She'd learned to deal with her ex-husband's taunting and hypocrisy much better than this careless display.

"Mommy?" came a voice through the phone.

Rebecca smiled broadly. "Abi!"

"Mommy! When are you coming back? I miss you."

"I'll be back soon, honey," Rebecca said. "Everything okay with Daddy?"

"Yeah, we're coloring and watching Sesame Street. Then we're getting a pizza."

"Great. I'll be home in a couple days. I love you, baby girl." Rebecca dabbed at her cheek.

John apparently had ended the call, and for a moment, Rebecca just stood there with the phone gripped in her hand. In the years since filing for divorce, she'd not felt one moment of regret. It was best for both herself and Abi. Still, when he offered, she didn't want to deprive Abi of having her father in her life. That old, naïve part of her still hoped he'd change and that this time would be different. This incident only further proved to her that she made the right choice—about the divorce, at least. She steadied herself, exhaled, and walked back into the restaurant.

Gwen Q and JJ watched her enter and seemed to read the conversation in her expression.

"That was John, wasn't it?" Gwen Q said, touching her shoulder.

Rebecca gave an affirming nod.

JJ raised her chin. "Whatever he said, try not to let it bother you, Rebecca. He has always been a small man and tries to shrink everyone down with him."

Rebecca tried to keep a brave face, but her voice broke a little as she said, "I know."

Gwen Q was still touching her shoulder. "You are an incredible woman, mother, and friend. That's all I have ever known you to be.

Don't let him twist the truth into a pretzel. Whatever he said, it isn't true."

Rebecca nodded purposefully to herself. "I know."

A waitress appeared with a trio of glasses and a large pitcher.

"Sangria," the waitress announced with a smile as she poured out three glasses of the ruby red liquid. "Freshly made."

JJ gave her a wink. "We figured you might need a little pick-me-up when you were finished on the phone."

Rebecca blinked. "How did you know it was John?"

"The look on your face when you saw the caller ID," Gwen Q said.

JJ nodded. "Besides, you hardly ever take calls in private—except when he's the one calling."

Rebecca nodded as she raised a glass. "Thank you. You guys are the best."

As she drained her fruity sangria, she thought how her friends really *were* the best. They were talented and beautiful and smart and kind but above all, in the several months since they'd found their bond again, their loyalty stood out. With JJ and Gwen Q at her side, she felt sure of herself. Whenever she let John cause her to doubt herself, they were always there to set her straight.

"So," she said, clearing her throat. "What's the plan for tonight?"

JJ gave an encouraging smile. "Tony's working on getting some information on the Monza. If he succeeds, then we'll be heading there tonight."

Rebecca nodded, impressed. "And what's the plan when we get to this secret place?"

"Right. I've been thinking about it. Bruce Balvin is our primary target. Q, I think you should initiate contact with him. Try to get information any way you can. He won't speak to me."

Gwen Q shrugged. "I'll try."

JJ gave a satisfied nod. "Good."

"What's good?" came a voice from behind them.

They glanced around to find Tony, who was grinning as he strode toward their table.

"Please tell us you have some good news," JJ said, gesturing to the waitress to bring another glass.

Tony grinned. "I certainly do." He slid Ted Cookie's card with the address and number across the table. Rebecca took the card, entered the address into her phone, and began to work.

JJ grinned. "How on earth did you manage that?"

"A bit of flattery," he said. "Turns out that Ted Cookie has quite the ego. Just the thought of being treated like a kingpin was enough to get him on our side."

"He'll get us in tonight?" JJ asked.

Tony nodded. "I already called and have the password."

"Nice!" Gwen Q said, wide-eyed. "What is it?"

Tony leaned forward, lowering his voice. "Diamonds."

"Excellent work," JJ said. "We need to make sure we maximize this opportunity. It might be the only chance we get to go inside the Monza. It sounds like a potentially dangerous place, and we have to pull this off without a glitch."

"Okay." Rebecca held up her phone screen and pointed. "So, right here, across the street from the Monza is a local pizza place. I suggest we have someone stationed there to do surveillance on the ins and outs of the club."

JJ nodded. "Makes sense. I think you should do the honors."

Rebecca gave a start. "Me?"

"You're the best for the job," JJ said with a confident nod. "Vigilant, meticulous, and master of high-tech surveillance."

Rebecca appreciated the compliment, and she did agree with JJ's logic, but she still wondered if this was JJ's way of keeping her out of the action. Any talk of John always brought to mind the fact that Rebecca was the only one who had a child. She had responsibilities that Gwen Q and JJ did not and sometimes Rebecca worried they protected her because of it. This time, however, she wouldn't protest —she *was* the best person for this job.

She met JJ's eye. "Let's do it."

CHAPTER 15

*G*wen Q had her hair pulled back and her street cool vibe on as they walked through Fremont Street. Her heart thumped with every step. She was on a stealth mission and knew she could pull it off, but dangerous places like the Monza still put her on edge. But they all had the same challenge—staying cool while outside of their comfort zones. Tony and JJ walked beside her and seemed to radiate similar levels of both focus and apprehension as they approached the given address.

The Monza bar was a low-key spot located on the basement floor of what appeared to be an antique store.

A bulky man, dressed in a dark T-shirt with the giveaway sign of an earpiece drooping from his lobe, stood protectively at the bar door.

Gwen Q flashed him a smile as they approached, and his jaw clenched slightly as he appeared to stop himself from smiling back.

He gave the three of them an appraising stare as he stood protectively in front of the door. "Password?"

Tony leaned forward. "Diamonds."

The bouncer continued to look them up and down, giving no sign he'd let them past.

"We're with the Cookie Monster," Tony added in a low voice.

SUSPICION ON THE STRIP

The bouncer had a suspicious look but stepped aside. "All right then. Enjoy your night." He held the door open.

Gwen Q felt her heartbeat slow down as she crossed the threshold inside. Her nervousness was fading and being replaced with her signature easy flow. The goal was blissfully straightforward. *Find Bruce Balvin and make him talk.*

Jazz music wafted from somewhere unseen and patrons moved about with practiced ease—they were regulars. It was dimly lit, boasted a long, wooden bar, and was furnished like a prohibition-era speakeasy. The colors were mahogany and rouge, including the tiled ceiling. One quick glance around brought a smile to Gwen Q's face. She knew exactly what she needed to do.

She sauntered breezily to the bar and climbed onto a stool at the corner of the bar counter. The natural instinct might have been to take a walk around the place, then decide where to sit, but Gwen Q knew from experience that ambling without a clear destination made one look lost and unimportant in spaces like this. Bars like the Monza were akin to the jungle savannah—dominated by territory and prestige. The first order of business was to establish your territory—the second was to make your territory prestigious.

In a quick glance, Gwen Q had discerned that the private booths looked like unclaimable territory, so the bar was the next best option. Perched atop her barstool, she took her first real look around. A stage at the center of the room featured a retro style burlesque dancer with make-up that gave her features an eccentric, exaggerated cast. Gwen Q realized then that the music came from a small orchestra of musicians stationed at the far corner of the room. Their music was smooth, butter-soft jazz. Subtle, solemn, but rousing and enthralling. The Monza was certainly relaxed, but this was no cheap joint. Upon closer look, Gwen guessed that the elegantly carved wood used for the bar counter was Brazilian rosewood.

Gwen Q gestured to the bartender. When their eyes met, she pointed at a bottle of cabernet and held up three fingers. The bartender smiled and nodded his understanding as a cool jazz piano played.

By the time Tony and JJ were seated beside her, the waiter had produced the chosen bottle with three delicate wine glasses.

"Bruce Balvin will be in the cigar room," Gwen Q said.

Tony glanced at her. "The cigar room?"

Gwen Q nodded. "Over your shoulder to the right. The small door with the Incredible Hulk standing outside."

Tony looked over his shoulder and squinted. "I see it. How do you know he's in there?"

Gwen Q took a sip of cabernet. "You can tell by the booths here. A lot of men, too much whiskey on the tables. All posturing for one another. Here to be seen. The sort of men we're looking for don't have to posture—and they don't want to be seen. They'll be in the private spaces, and judging by the size of that bouncer's bicep, I'll bet that cigar room is gonna be pretty private tonight."

Tony nodded, appearing impressed by Gwen's split-second analysis. He seemed to be confirming the size of the bouncers. "How do we get in?"

JJ chuckled and touched Tony's shoulder. "I think Gwen can take it from here."

Gwen Q finished her wine and rose from the bar stool. She winked at Tony. "Be back soon."

She walked straight for the cigar room. Now, historically, a smile, a few whispered words, and a hair flip were enough for Gwen Q to charm any bouncer and unlock the doors of any nightlife establishment. But the truth was, despite her seeming unflappable confidence, Gwen had felt adrift since her mother died several years back, and it was mainly due to her reunion with JJ and Rebecca that her natural self-assurance had been restored. Still, even at her best, the Monza was a unique venue, and there was no guarantee that the behemoth guarding the cigar room would let her past. This entire piece of the investigation rode on her success in the next few moments. The bouncer just had to let her through.

The imposing man did not hide his lengthy appraisal of Gwen. She kept her easy cool. This was her territory, and she had to come across like she owned the place. In the moment of truth, any faltering in her confidence was fatal.

She stepped closer and could almost feel his hot breath at the side of her neck. Then she strolled past him, pointedly ignoring him as though he was a pillar of cement rather than a gargantuan human being. He met her glance for a whisper of a second, appearing taken back by her audacious assurance. Her glance was granite.

The bouncer hesitated and crossed his arms in front of him. Perhaps in spite of himself, he stepped aside, pulling the velvet rope away. He didn't ask for a name or a password. Nothing. She'd made him believe she belonged. As she strode past the velvet rope, she breathed out a sigh of relief. *Now I just have to find Bruce Balvin.*

* * *

Tony finished his wine as he watched Gwen Q somehow walk straight into the cigar room.

"How did she do that?"

"Oh, that? It's a gift." JJ smiled and shook her head. "Like her innate superpower that you can't exactly break down into its component parts."

"I see. Impressive."

His eyes met JJ's for a moment and he felt a sharp swell in his chest. He knew it wasn't just the wine. JJ just looked incredible. He had always thought so since the first day he'd met her when she was dressed in a kitchen apron with tomato sauce and oil smeared all over it. Though her gymnastics days were behind her, she'd retained the trim, toned physique that shone through whatever she wore. But her attractiveness came from a much deeper place as well. JJ had heart, smarts, courage, talent, and passion.

"I wasn't sure what to expect, but this place is really nice." She took a swig of her cabernet. "Crime really does pay." She laughed.

Tony's smile faded. "It doesn't really. Not in the end."

"I'm kidding. Why so serious?"

"Just family stuff."

"Okay..."

He was silent a long moment before he spoke. "My uncle was once part of the Cipriani crime family. Back in the eighties."

"Oh, really?" JJ said, leaning toward him.

He caught a whiff of her perfume and it proved more intoxicating to him than the wine. Gathering himself, he continued his story. "He was an underboss, second only to the Don himself. I don't know if he actually, you know... hurt anyone, but some days he would get really quiet and sit by himself for hours at a time. My cousins didn't have a relationship with him. He sent them to all these great schools and bought them sports cars, but they left and went as far away as they could the first chance they got. He married into the family. He's not a Natale. But now he's out here and alone. The whole extended family feels he so disgraced our name that basically everyone avoids talking about him. Like he's not even there anymore."

JJ furrowed her brow. "Wow, that's... that's really sad."

Tony lowered his chin. "I'm sorry. I didn't mean to kill the mood."

JJ shook her head and touched his wrist. "No, you don't have to apologize." She hesitated. "You know, I always wonder if people would do things differently if they had it to do all over again. Realize that money and power aren't really worth it. Heck, it's easy for us normal people to have regrets. Can you imagine if you're a crime boss?"

"True." Tony nodded. "As for my uncle, I'll bet he would. It's like at a certain juncture years ago he took a crooked road. Then there was no coming back."

They locked eyes for a moment of companionable silence and Tony felt in that moment that JJ understood him like he'd never felt understood before.

"We should move around a little," JJ said, breaking up the silence. "See if we can find any information."

Tony straightened. "Yeah, of course."

"I think it will be less suspicious if we pretend we're a couple. You generally wouldn't come to this sort of place alone."

Tony nodded. "Of course. Right."

They walked to another corner of the bar arm-in-arm and struck up a conversation with a slightly older couple at the corner who were enjoying a bottle of champagne. Only two minutes of conversation were enough to know this couple would be no help to the investigation. Even so, for some reason, JJ and Tony kept talking to them.

It turned out that the Monza bar wasn't just for criminals but also for discerning patrons who knew it was a place for exclusivity and privacy. The couple, Katherine and James, probably in their fifties, were on their honeymoon, having been married in Las Vegas just the week before. From his Rolex and her enormous rock, it was obvious they had money. When they asked Tony and JJ what they did, the two answered half-honestly. Tony explained that he worked for a real estate company, and JJ added that she worked as a chef at a Greek restaurant. That led to a discussion about Greek food—a subject evoking unanimous enthusiasm.

After near twenty minutes of conversation, Tony and JJ said their goodbyes and returned to the bar.

"Nice people," JJ said.

"Very nice," Tony agreed.

JJ raised her chin. "I have a theory on the person responsible for Winona's death."

"Go on," said Tony.

"I think the thief wanted to kill Winona. I don't think it was just a matter of chance or necessity. I think it was part of the job."

Tony's eyebrows rose. "Why do you think that?"

"Just thinking back on how I didn't see any signs of a struggle or violence. You would have thought she was sleeping. Killing someone that way doesn't happen by chance. It takes planning."

"So, in other words, we're looking for someone who had reason to kill Winona, not just steal the Arapaho?"

JJ nodded. "That's what I think."

"So," Tony said, cupping his chin. "The question is, why would anyone want to kill a nice person like Winona Dakota?"

"Because she was an obstacle."

CHAPTER 16

Gwen Q had seen Bruce Balvin only once in a photograph that Rebecca had managed to unearth in her research into the heavy-hitters in high stakes betting. She was looking for a heavy, balding man with eyes like big, dark shirt buttons. She glanced at the faces in the cigar room. None of them even looked close to the man in Rebecca's picture.

"Looking for someone?" came a raspy voice.

Gwen Q stopped short and glanced over at the bearded man wearing a silk shirt that was unbuttoned all the way to the navel. He smiled curiously at her and raised his chin, exposing the tattoo across his neck with the word Liberty in dark ink. He had twin gold chains around his neck and hair that fell past his shoulders like he was in a 90s rock band. *Wait, he actually was in a rock band.*

"You're Luke the Stickman," she said honestly. "The drummer."

He gave half a bow. "Guilty as charged." He glanced up at her with a nervous grin playing at the corners of his mouth and looked around. "You here with anybody?"

Gwen Q touched her neck. In a room full of criminals, it was an act of personal safety on his part to know who was accompanying a woman before he proceeded to flirt with her. She had to play that to her advantage.

She tilted her head back and smiled playfully. "Who do you think I'm here with?"

He grinned at her, then gazed around the room, his eyes landing on a young goon of a guy with slicked-back hair. "Well, you're too . . . sophisticated to be here with Joe Roth."

Gwen Q laughed. "You mean I'm too old."

He raised his hands in self-defense. "Didn't say that."

"You didn't have to."

He continued searching. "Not Lorenzo either."

Gwen Q smiled and offered him her elbow. "How about you forget about who I came with and introduce me to people I want to know."

His eyebrows rose. "A woman who goes after what she wants." He curled a hand around her elbow and led her past the first table, speaking quietly enough for only her to hear. "That's the Bardicci family. They run a small casino on the Strip. Old money that's running out." He proceeded to the second table. "Tom Johnson and his brother James. Tom's got a son who's a world champion cage fighter." He gestured to the third table with his chin. "The Kleinmans, the aforementioned Joe Roth, and some guy from Pennsylvania."

Gwen Q narrowed her eyes at that, inspecting the third table. Bruce Balvin sat at the head of the table guzzling a preposterous plate of calamari. He seemed very relaxed, which Gwen Q assumed had something to do with the empty champagne bottles perched upside down in a large ice bucket that dominated the table. Their eyes met briefly, but Balvin offered no hint of recognition as he took a long drag from his fat cigar and blew out a bulbous cloud of smoke.

Luke the Stickman stopped short of the fourth table. "So, if it's not any one of those guys, either I'm in luck or . . ." He glanced at the fourth table. "Or I'm all *out* of luck because you're here with Frank Gunn."

Frank Gunn, a short, squatty man, sat at the head of a corner table. He was dressed in a double-breasted black suit touched with a gold pocket square. Though he was surrounded by drinks and large, menacing people, he looked utterly bored by it all. There was something clearly dangerous about the man. In the way people kept space around him. How his suit was loose-fitting enough to conceal a weapon. He seemed to be a gangster of the old, forgotten variety. The real deal.

"No," Gwen Q said, "I'm not here with Frank Gunn."

"Good. In his business, people tend to turn up missing, if you know what I mean," Luke said, looking up at the crowd.

"Missing? Like dead?" Gwen Q fought to keep her casual tone.

"With enough dough, you can contract Gunn's goons for just about anything. Hits, drugs, you name it." Luke the Stickman straightened and returned his gaze to Gwen Q. "So you're here alone, then?"

She shook her head. "Not quite." She turned to glance at Bruce Balvin. "I'm from Pennsylvania."

She smiled at Luke, then turned directly toward Bruce Balvin's table. The man glanced up as soon as her shadow fell over his plate of calamari. Their eyes met, and Gwen Q felt she could see the wheels turning in his head.

She slid into the space beside him. "You're not from here, are you?"

He chewed a piece of calamari to smithereens before turning to directly look at her. "How can you tell?"

She flashed a smile. "Are you here on business or pleasure?"

He gave a leering grin that made Gwen Q's stomach lurch. "Always a bit of both."

She managed to eke out a return smile. She had hoped he wouldn't try to flirt but luck comes and goes as it pleases. "Tell me about both. Business first."

Balvin squinted as he studied her, and for a moment, Gwen Q felt terribly vulnerable, being reminded in that instant that she was in a room full of criminals, many of whom were likely armed and could easily bundle her out through some back-alley door and into a van never to be seen again.

"I'm looking into the hospitality business." Bruce pushed his now-empty plate toward the middle of the table. "Trying to acquire a stake in the hotel and casino business."

"Oh, really?" Gwen Q feigned a fawning look of interest. "Which one?"

He hesitated and stared at her. "I can't say yet. Confidential for now. Until it's all official."

Gwen Q lowered her head. "Of course."

Bruce's phone illuminated beside the calamari plate, and they both instinctively glanced down. Gwen Q stifled a gasp. The caller ID read Rocky Neapolitan. *Who is Rocky Neapolitan?*

Balvin flipped the phone face down, ignored the call, and grabbed his champagne glass. As he did so, the phone started to ring again. He turned it over and let out an exasperated sigh.

"I apologize," he said, pushing his chair back. "Gotta take this."

She frowned. "Aww, so soon?"

He rose to his feet. "Afraid so."

Gwen Q frantically tried to recall the number of the disposable burner phone they brought with them on the trip for times such as this. *Does it end in four-three or three-four?*

"Aren't you going to take my number?" she asked, without standing up. "I'll even put it in for you."

He glanced at her and considered it for a moment. He wobbled slightly under the influence of too much champagne. "Sure." He held out his phone.

At a lightning-fast speed, she copied Rocky Neapolitan's number into a text and sent it to her real cell number. Then she dialed the code *#06# to reveal the phone's unique serial number and sent this information as well. Last of all, she deleted the texts she'd just sent, then created a new contact in Balvin's phone with what she prayed was their correct burner phone number. With a casual smile, she returned the phone. "Okay, there you go. My number's in there. You can call or text me, so then I'll have yours."

Bruce seemed intoxicated by both his drink and Gwen's charm. He glanced at the name she'd saved and nodded. "I will." He smiled. "Gloria."

She waited a good ten minutes after Bruce left before attempting her exit. Just as she approached the door of the cigar room, Luke the Stickman reappeared.

"Leaving so soon?" he asked.

Gwen faked a yawn and nodded. "Tired." She kept walking but he matched her stride, keeping an easy pace with her.

"Hey, if you dig a venue like this, I know one you'd really like," he said with a wink.

She turned to him and grinned. "Really?"

He nodded. "An underground boxing club. Every weekend. But not just boxing. Some pretty radical events. Some on the violent side, but other tamer stuff, too. Like private shows from top rockers. High-end art auctions."

"Really?" Gwen Q stopped in her tracks. *Art auctions?* She tried to sound as casual as possible. "How did you know I had a thing for art?"

Clearly pleased with Gwen Q's reaction, Luke the Stickman gave more away. "Lucky guess. I've heard that native sculpture might even be there tomorrow. You know, the one that was stolen at the Neapolitan."

Gwen Q blinked. "I'm not sure I know what you're talking about."

"Some big deal Native American sculpture. The one that was swiped from Winona Dakota."

Gwen feigned realization. "Oh, right, the talk show host. I heard something on the news about that."

"Yup. Word on the street is that they have it, and it'll be there at the auction. Someone's about to make some serious dough."

"How interesting," Gwen Q said, summoning all her powers of patience and restraint to stop the ever-growing list of questions from spilling out of her mouth all at once. She stole a breath and said innocently, "So, where is this underground place?"

Luke shook his head and shot a cocky smile. "It's a secret until right before the event. I could finagle a plus one for someone cool. But once you're in, the doors close until the end. Give me your number and we'll meet up. Usually a swanky party going on, too."

Gwen Q delivered a cat-like smile as she entered, for the second time that night, what she hoped was the correct fake number.

Luke flashed a triumphant smile in return. "You're quite a catch, Gloria."

Gwen Q smiled and strode out of the cigar room. As she brushed past the velvet rope she glanced up at the bouncer and waved.

JJ and Tony were waiting at the bar. They could tell by Gwen's expression that things had gone well. Gwen sat a couple seats down the bar so as not to look conspicuous. JJ smiled and pointed at her, mouthing, *You still got it.*

CHAPTER 17

JJ, Tony, and Gwen Q exited the Monza and headed to the pizza shop across the street, where they linked up with Rebecca.

"I found something, guys," Rebecca announced. "Something that might be big."

"Me, too," Gwen Q added.

Gwen and Rebecca both looked at JJ and Tony, who were silent.

"Sorry," JJ said, laughing. "We got nothin'."

They walked to the corner of Fremont Street where Tony hailed a cab and they headed back to the Neapolitan. The drive was brief, and they instinctively moved to their unofficial headquarters, the museum café, as soon as they arrived.

"You go first, Q," Rebecca urged, as they sat down at one of the many empty tables.

Gwen Q began to unravel her story, telling of her encounter with Bruce Balvin, how they'd exchanged numbers, and that he had received a call from someone named Rocky Neapolitan. She went on to divulge how Balvin was trying to get involved in some hotel business on the Strip and. "And..."

"There's more?" JJ asked.

"I also got his phone's serial number," Gwen Q added with a smile, turning to Rebecca. "Like you showed me that day back in the Batcave."

"His IMEI number? That's my girl." Rebecca grinned and flipped open her small travel laptop. "This is a game-changer."

Tony raised an eyebrow, a little confused. "Could someone please explain?"

Rebecca turned her screen around as a series of black and white binary codes rushed up and down the screen like something out of *The Matrix*. "I have access to the cellular network provider databases and can match names to IMEI numbers."

"What's an IMEI number?" he asked.

"Every phone has one," Rebecca explained. "It stands for International Mobile Equipment Identity. It's like a license plate for cell phones. Every time you make a call or text, your phone sends a signal to the nearest cell tower when in range. It's why they're called cell phones. Every phone needs a cell tower within range to operate."

Tony nodded. "I see."

"With an IMEI number, we can track location pretty accurately. Monitor calls. Texts. We can even initiate calls and texts remotely."

Tony stood back, looking impressed. "That's incredible."

Rebecca winked. "You haven't seen the half of it."

"And . . ." Gwen continued.

"More?" Tony asked with a stupefied look.

Gwen nodded. "I met Luke the Stickman, and—"

"The drummer from like years ago, with the hair?" Rebecca asked, incredulous.

"Right." As Gwen Q continued, their mouths fell open when she got to the part where the rocker had invited her to an illicit auction where the Arapaho was rumored to go on sale.

JJ listened to Gwen Q's account with the patient attention of a hawk, her eyes wide with calculation as she considered what that bombshell meant to their investigation. "You said you found something big, too, Rebecca. What was it?"

Rebecca leaned forward in her seat as she described Ted Cookie's arrival at the Monza just before midnight, and how the bouncer gave him a wad of cash in exchange for what looked like a baggie, presumably containing drugs. The two then proceeded to operate out of the alley adjacent to the club door to a variety of 'customers' all night—running the gamut from clean-cut, inebriated types in tuxedoes, to the sleaziest in town, and everything in between.

Her second discovery— the real news—was discovered while researching on her phone when the activity had grown idle in the alleyway.

"I was looking into that man from the picture we saw in Reno. With the handlebar mustache," Rebecca began.

JJ raised an eyebrow. "Jacobi Dakota?"

Rebecca nodded. "Right. I was reading through his tribute page on forevermissed.com and saw a post from someone who called him 'Dad.'"

JJ gave a start. "Did you get a name?"

"Not quite. The post was made with the sign-off *A.M.*, so I started to run through names with those initials. I didn't have much luck with that, so I went back to the site to see if anyone else posted anything that looked like a lead. There was a message that caught my eye from someone named Eliza Malka." She picked up her phone. "This Eliza posted a message that read: *To the one I love the most. You'll never be forgotten.*"

"Hmm," JJ mused. "Sounds like a lover."

Rebecca nodded. "So I checked her out, and apparently, she lives in Reno with her son Alex."

"Alex," Gwen Q said aloud. "A.M."

"Where did we hear that name before?" JJ mused.

Rebecca nodded. "I looked up Alex Malka and . . ." She held up her phone to the group.

The image on her screen was of a thirty-something man, slender and dark-haired—with a thick, handlebar mustache. A cold shiver of recognition hit JJ like a wave. "That's him."

"There's more. Turns out Alex Malka was arrested five years ago for—get this—attempted robbery of an armored van."

Tony gaped. "No way."

JJ gave a knowing nod. "He's our guy. It has to be him. That's where we heard the name before. He was on that staff list that Montell gave us."

"It's all there," Gwen Q added. "Motive, means, and opportunity. He has to be him."

Tony nodded. "How do we find him?"

"Well, his last known address was at a motel in Reno, not far from where the Dakotas live," Rebecca said.

"Incredible work, Watson," JJ said.

"All in your service, Sherlock," Rebecca said with a chuckle.

"We have to go to the police with this, right away." JJ's expression grew serious. "He's our man."

Rebecca's face fell, her excitement fading. "What? I thought you were going to say we're heading to Reno."

JJ shook her head. "We can't just go after a suspected criminal. It's too dangerous. We have to leave it to the police this time."

Gwen Q nodded. "I agree."

Rebecca sighed. "Fine."

"I'll make the call now," JJ said, fishing her phone from her pocket.

"Now? It's three in the morning," Rebecca said.

"Hey, they said to call with any leads 24/7." JJ tapped the number.

There was an answer on the first ring.

"Tyrell."

Oh, of course she'd answer. JJ cleared her throat, surprised by how quickly the answer had come. "Hello, Officer Tyrell. This is Julia Kamaras. We met last week."

Tyrell let out an irritated-sounding sigh. "I know who you are."

"I'm calling with information on the fatal robbery at the Neapolitan," JJ said.

"Go on."

JJ proceeded to tell Officer Tyrell everything, leading all the way up to her final revelation that they had identified Alex Malka as the man with the handlebar mustache she had spotted near the scene of the crime just moments after it must have happened.

There was silence on the other end of the line for a long moment.

"Officer Tyrell? Are you still there?"

Tyrell did not sound happy. "I'm still here."

"And you heard everything that I said?"

"I did," Officer Tyrell said. "Is that all the information you have?"

JJ blinked and frowned. "Right now it is."

"Well then, Miss Kamaras, I'll try to be as clear as I can be here. This is a police investigation. A real one. You are a civilian. Calling with a lead is one thing. We take it from there. I told you to stay out of our way, but apparently, I must be even more crystal clear. If I catch you near this case again, I'll have you arrested on obstruction of justice."

"What?" JJ bellowed. "The investigation is over. We solved it. What more information do you need?"

"We've already been in touch with Mr. Malka. He's not responsible."

"How do you know?"

"Because we have the toxicology report, the autopsy, and other confidential information that you are not privy to."

JJ raised her voice. "He was probably the last person to see her alive."

"Not exactly," Tyrell hissed. "You were."

"Excuse me?"

"The autopsy suggests she was still alive when you allegedly found her unconscious in her room."

"Are you saying I'm the prime suspect now?"

"I am saying you should stay out of our investigation, and leave this to the professionals. This isn't Jim Thorpe. Your little detective certificate means squat here. So, take your small town, Agatha Christie nonsense back home and stay there. We have a real investigation to conduct."

"But—"

Tyrell ended the call. JJ dropped the phone, her chest heaving.

"What happened?" Rebecca asked.

JJ was too angry to speak.

"What just went down, JJ?" Gwen Q added.

She pushed her chair out from the table and hesitated. "Tyrell isn't interested in Alex as a suspect. She says they have spoken to him already, and he's clean. Warned me to stay out of it."

Rebecca blinked. "Are you going to listen to them?"

JJ's jaw tightened. "Heck, no."

Rebecca grinned. "Okay, so let's hear it."

JJ stood up with resolve in her eyes. "Tomorrow, we're going to Reno."

CHAPTER 18

*R*ebecca and JJ sat in Noah's Lincoln Navigator on their way to Reno, Nevada. Gwen Q and Tony had stayed behind to investigate the secret auction, Rocky Neapolitan, and the involvement of Bruce Balvin. Tony mentioned he knew someone on the force and would try to get a copy of the autopsy and toxicology reports.

The sun was at its noonday peak when they drove past a triumphal arch that read *Reno: The Biggest Little City in the World*. The motel in question was at the corner of a long strip mall, right beside a drive-thru Taco Bell. They parked on the dusty street and climbed out of the vehicle.

JJ had to admit that Lexington Motel was cleaner and more inviting than anyone would have expected from the outside. It had a classic, wood-paneled façade, modern windows on all three stories, a front desk area that boasted clean, if dated, couches and a sign that advertised room prices beginning at $52 a night.

The sitting area was carpeted in deep purple shag. A housekeeper strode by wearing a purple uniform as she pushed along a wheeled, metallic mop bucket. Ornamental fake flowers—also purple— sat on the front desk, but the air smelled fresh with a hint of cleaning solution, which could have been worse.

JJ approached the reception desk and rang the bell.

A small Polynesian man with a ponytail appeared. "Hello, may I help you?"

"We're here to visit someone."

He flinched and gave her an appraising look. "Do you know the person's room number?"

JJ shook her head. "I'm afraid not."

He frowned. "I don't think I can offer much help then. You'll have to give them a call and ask for the room number."

"Alex Malka," JJ said, raising her voice above the clang of the housekeeper's mop and bucket down the corridor. "Some people call him A.M."

The man blinked and crossed his arms. "What do you want with him?"

"We just want to talk, that's all."

"Well, if it's A.M. you want, I definitely can't help you. I'm looking for him myself. Haven't seen him in three days." The man frowned. "Owes me at least a month's rent. If you find him, tell him I said he better have my money with interest. He was out in room 232, but he only comes by when he knows I can't catch him."

JJ glanced at Rebecca, who gave her a slight nod.

"So it's been at least three days since he's been here?"

The man stood back and glared at JJ. "Are you some kind of cop? If he's got himself into trouble, I've got no parts of it. You can check my entire establishment. We've got all our permits and everything. He waved an accusing finger at JJ. "This is no five-star establishment, but it's an honest business we have here."

"We aren't cops," JJ said calmly, "and I must say, you have a nice place here, Mr.—" She squinted to make out the name on his identification tag. "Tiare. It's clean, welcoming, and well-priced—so, five-star or not, looks like you know good hospitality. I'm in the hospitality business myself—the restaurant business. I can always spot quality."

Tiare's face shifted from a deep frown to a faint smile. "Thank you." He hesitated before remembering her question. "Well, I don't remember exactly what day I saw him, but A.M. and his friends are always out by the pool on the weekends. They're there until the early hours of the morning usually or until someone threatens to call the police."

"And they were there last weekend?"

Tiare blinked and glanced at the ceiling. "I think so."

JJ nodded. "Mr. Tiare, do you mind if we take a look around and see if we spot him anywhere?"

He shrugged. "Be my guest. Room 232 is round the back way. Right behind the swimming pool."

JJ flashed a smile. "Thank you. My name is Julia by the way. Julia Kamaras."

He nodded. "A pleasure to meet you, Julia."

They walked back out through the automatic doors and around the back, following the arrows pointing in the direction of the swimming pool. Several chairs were clustered around a plastic table with an ashtray in the center, and JJ had a hunch that was the place Alex Malka and friends had made their hangout spot. They found room 232 locked, dark, and quiet.

"He isn't here," Rebecca said quietly. "Maybe he left."

JJ shook her head. "Nah, he's still here."

"How do you know?" Rebecca asked.

JJ pointed at the grass hedge just beside the door. One of the plants dangled in the wind, appearing freshly broken. "Someone has been walking through this way to get to their room. Probably in the dark."

Rebecca nodded. "He's been sneaking back in at night."

"Yup," JJ said.

"So do we wait until he—"

They both froze as the sound of footsteps carried on the wind. They turned in the direction of the sound and saw a man come into view, perhaps returning from what must have been a trip to the grocery store. He was tall and broader at the shoulder than JJ had expected but he had the handlebar mustache, the carved chin, and the dark hair. He was Jacobi Dakota's son for sure—a chip off the old block.

The man was about to cut through the grass when he noticed JJ and Rebecca. Their eyes locked for a brief moment, then he froze, dropped his shopping bags, and took off running.

JJ and Rebecca exchanged frantic glances.

"Okay, Pride of Pan Am," Rebecca said. "This is your department."

JJ took a deep breath and sprinted after him.

CHAPTER 19

*J*J's heart was pounding in her chest as she leaped over the rear wall. She pressed forward, taking it up a notch to top speed. With every cheetah-like stride, the sound of Alex Malka's panting grew louder.

"I got you," she whispered. Though he had a substantial head start, she was gaining on him.

The dark-haired man changed direction as JJ closed in on him. A low iron fence several yards away came into view. Alex cleared the fence—barely—in a single, running bound. JJ grinned as she closed in on the gate. Now, this was fun. With a dancer's flourish and without breaking her stride, she split-leaped over the fence with ease, landing in a full run. Alex glanced back in a panic over his shoulder. He looked shocked to see she was still coming.

They came at last to the corner of the motel. There was only one place to go from there—the freeway. She couldn't let it get to that. JJ gritted her teeth and pushed harder. She inched closer to him, grabbed the back of his shirt, and swung him around.

"Okay!" he shouted, holding a hand up in surrender. "Get off me, lady!"

They were just beside Noah's car where Alex stood doubled over with hands on hips and blowing hard, looking like he might pass out.

JJ glared at him, gathering her breath as she did so, but still remained cautious. Though the man seemed ready to keel over, he was still potentially a dangerous criminal.

"What . . . are . . . you," Alex hissed, through heavy breaths as she closed in on him. "Some kind of . . . Cyborg?"

JJ circled him, one hand gripped on the pepper spray her father had insisted she bring on their trip. One wrong move and she would douse him to oblivion.

"What are you chasing me for?" he snarled. "I told Tiare already I'll get him his money."

At this point, JJ had to admit, he looked harmless. "This isn't about Tiare."

"Huh?" Still panting, he wiped sweat from his brow. "Why the four-minute mile then?"

JJ hesitated, curling her hand tighter around the pepper spray. She glanced over her shoulder slightly and saw Rebecca coming around the corner. "It's about the Neapolitan."

"What?" Alex's face fell, and he shook his head. "I told the cops everything already. I wasn't involved. I just worked there as a janitor. I had no idea what went on."

"Then why were you on Winona's floor moments after it happened?"

"I told you, it wasn't me," he snapped. "Look," he reached for something in the pocket of his hoodie, and JJ wasted no time.

She squeezed the pepper spray canister until it was sputtered dry. Alex screamed and went down clutching his face. Only then did JJ realize what he was holding. Not a gun, not a knife, but an ID Card. She read it slowly. Alex Malka. Janitor. The Neapolitan Hotel and Casino.

"What the heck did you do that for?" he yelled, squirming on the ground.

JJ raised her hands apologetically. "I'm so sorry."

Just then, Rebecca appeared beside her and started spraying him too. "Eat this!" she shouted as she hit him with another burst.

"Rebecca stop!" JJ warned, holding her hand out.

"Why?" Rebecca lowered her pepper spray slowly. "I thought he tried to attack you."

"Not exactly."

Rebecca watched Alex squirm like a salted slug on the ground. "What do we do?"

JJ looked left and right. "Go get Noah. We have to take him to a hospital."

* * *

A FEW HOURS LATER, JJ and Alex Malka sat around a table at Taco Bell. Pop music was playing on the speakers, and the bulbs in the closest light fixture flickered above them.

Alex picked up his fat burrito and hungrily took a bite. Though JJ had not totally dismissed him as their prime suspect, she had the increasing impression that Alex Malka was not the sort to murder.

Rebecca appeared with a super-sized soda and put it down beside him. "There you go."

Alex took another bite from the burrito, gulped down a good mouthful of soda, and let out an exultant "Ahhh."

JJ waited for him to finish before she spoke.

"I'm sorry again for pepper spraying you. I thought you had a gun."

He glanced up from his meal. "I told you. I'm not a criminal. Well, anymore. And I never hurt anyone even then."

"Okay." JJ nodded. "So why don't you tell me who you actually are?"

He blinked. "Ladies first. You're the ones who showed up at *my* doorstep."

JJ glanced at Rebecca and nodded. "Fair enough. My name is Julia, and I'm a private investigator. This is my colleague, Rebecca."

Alex took a noisy slurp of soda and nodded. "And you came all the way to Reno looking for me?"

JJ nodded. "I saw you the day Winona died. Near the elevator."

"I wasn't supposed to be there." Alex lowered his head. "I don't usually work that floor, but Winona called me to come look at her air conditioning unit. When I went to check it out, somehow it had been set on high, and the room was like a refrigerator."

"I see." JJ pulled a small notepad from her back pocket and scribbled. "Why were you in such a rush to leave?"

"People there don't like me. I have a criminal record, but they reluctantly hired me. If any of the bigwigs saw me on a floor where I wasn't assigned, I knew they'd think I was up to something, so I was trying to hustle out of there."

"Do you know the other employees in maintenance?" JJ asked.

"A few, but it's a huge hotel. Like its own city. There are loads of guys in maintenance I've never met." He watched JJ write and looked at her with a confused expression. "But the police already interviewed the hotel staff. I've been through this twice already."

"I told you, I'm not with the police, Alex. I'm just trying to help figure out what happened."

His eyes softened a bit as he took another slurp from his drink.

"Was there anything unusual about that day?" JJ asked. "Anything you can remember?"

He sat for a moment then shook his head. "Besides going to the seventh floor for the air conditioning, no. It was just a normal day."

"You said Winona called you directly to look at her air conditioning unit. She must have known you. Trusted you."

"Yeah, I don't know, maybe."

JJ studied him for a long moment. "We know that Winona Dakota was related to you."

He narrowed his eyes. "Who told you that?"

"Is that why you work at the Neapolitan?"

He was silent for a long moment as if wondering if he should answer. "Yes. Winnie . . ." He stopped and started to choke up. "Winnie got me the job. My mom and Jacobi, my dad, were never married. He'd come to visit us from time to time but we were never part of the *real* family, if you know what I mean. I was never a Dakota. Just had my mom's name. My mother never gave up on him, but I moved on a long time ago."

"Seems you carried on the handlebar mustache look."

"Yeah. I don't know why. Doesn't make much sense, does it?"

"Sure, it does," JJ said softly. "He was your dad."

Alex let out a humorless chuckle. "That's what Winnie used to say. She was so kind to me. The only one who accepted me, really. She kept in touch and sent me money a few times, called me on Christmas and my birthday. It meant a lot to me. She was a really special person. I wouldn't hurt her. No way. Never."

JJ bit down on her lip. She hated to admit it, but she believed Alex. There was an air of sincerity in his words that she couldn't deny. Still, something was missing from the picture. A piece that felt like it was stuck in her mind's blind spot. There were too many coincidences over the last several days to be the product of pure chance. There was foul play and she had to find out who was behind it.

JJ looked at him squarely. "So, what do *you* think happened?"

He sat in silence for a moment, staring at the remains of his burrito, and then rolled his shoulders into a reluctant shrug. "I really don't know. I wish I did. I wish I knew something that could help but the honest truth is that I don't. I'm sorry."

JJ glanced at Rebecca, but she had no questions either. They had pepper sprayed the man half to blindness, ruined his shirt, and questioned him mercilessly.

"So, now that Winona's gone, will you stay there at the Neapolitan?"

"No. Without her, I knew they'd try to get rid of me. So, I got a job at another hotel that, let's just say, isn't as picky about your past—the Golden Penny."

"I see." She slid a business card across the table to him. "Here's my card. If anything, anything at all, comes to mind about what happened, you give me a call."

He nodded. "I will."

JJ rose to her feet. "I promise we will do whatever we can to find out what happened to Winona." She shook his hand and smiled at him. "The mustache looks good on you."

CHAPTER 20

Tony knocked on the hospital room door, not sure what he'd find.

"Who is it?" came a low voice.

"Tony."

Tony heard footsteps approach the closed door, and when it opened, an unfamiliar man stood in the doorway.

Tony furrowed his brow. "I'm sorry, I thought this was my friend's room. I was sure it was room—"

"Come on in, Tone," came an instantly recognizable voice from behind the man. "It's okay. He's Rabbit's doctor."

The doctor smiled. "I was just on my way out." He turned back to Logan. "Remember, your friend needs to rest at least twenty-four hours."

"You got it, Doc," Logan called back.

The doctor walked out into the corridor, and Tony shut the door behind him.

Rabbit lay asleep on the bed closest to the window. Logan stood beside the curtains, with arms folded across his chest.

"He's doing well," Logan explained. "The doctor says he should be back to normal by tomorrow."

Tony stared at him. "That was—"

"I know it was, Tone," Logan said. "I know. It was a bonehead move."

Tony shook his head, "It's more than that, Logan."

Logan raised an eyebrow, his jaw set as though bracing for a punch. "What's it about then?"

"I know you've always been the wild man, but Maria's the real deal. She's an awesome woman and a good . . . anchor for you. She's been forgiving with your occasional party all-nighters, but she won't be forever. You could have lost her with a stunt like this."

"I know she's great. Look, I said it was irresponsible!"

"If Rabbit hadn't passed out so fast, you'd have tried the stuff, too. I don't want you to screw up your marriage before it even gets started."

"Yeah, then I'd still be single and forty—oh wait, like you."

Tony and Logan glared at each other for a long moment.

Then the tension cut as they both broke out laughing. Tony's perpetual singledom—his "priest's life" as Logan termed it—had always been a favorite subject for jokes. The truth was, Tony had been close to marriage about ten years prior to a woman named Jennifer, but before proposing, he'd come to the realization that the relationship lacked the depth and real intimacy he was truly looking for.

"So what about you finding *your* anchor one of these days, Father Natale?"

"Hilarious." Tony hesitated. "Okay, fine. Yes, that would be nice."

"Why you broke up with that Jennifer is the mystery of the century. Girl was gorgeous. Great job. Somehow was crazy about you."

Tony let out a humorless chuckle. "Yeah, well, she wasn't … the one, okay?" His expression suddenly turned serious. "Something I wanted to ask you, Logan."

Logan stirred. "Shoot."

"Is your brother Victor still a cop?"

"Yeah, of course."

Tony nodded. "Do you think he could speak to someone with the Las Vegas police department for me?"

"Why?" Logan stepped closer. "Are you in trouble or something?"

"No, nothing like that. I'm trying to get information on something."

"Something like what?"

"The death of Winona Dakota."

"The talk show host? The one that died?"

Tony nodded. "Yeah."

"What for?

"It's just something . . . " Tony sighed. "Something I'm working on with a friend of mine."

Logan looked as though he wanted to ask more questions but instead retrieved his phone and called his brother. He passed the phone to Tony, and after a brief conversation, Victor promised to see if he could get copies of the information that Tony needed.

"How can I thank you, buddy?" Tony said when they ended the call.

"Oh, I have some ideas."

Tony smirked "I'm afraid to ask. What?"

"Let's get out of here and go to the casino. Gamble a little. Nothing crazy. But c'mon, we're in Vegas."

Tony nodded and gave a smile of agreement. "All right."

"Perf!" Logan said, clapping his hands. "Logue and Tone, back together again! Watch out!"

* * *

TWENTY MINUTES LATER, they were back at the Neapolitan on the basement level, staring over the gambling floor. Though the casino was not fully at capacity, there was still a hefty crowd that appeared fully consumed with gambling and drinking. The main room was decorated with gilded Grecian columns and enormous floor-to-ceiling mirrors. Elegant paintings of historic figures stared down approvingly from their perches on the wall. Without a window in sight, the room was lit exclusively by elaborate cut-glass chandeliers that carried a soft candlelight glow. The most expensive card tables were at the center of the casino, where people clustered in groups to watch the biggest spenders go at it—players who easily wagered thousands of dollars on each hand.

"Shall we?" Logan said, rubbing his hands, and heading for the roulette wheel. Tony nodded, and they sat at the roulette table after acquiring some drinks and a modest stack of chips. Tony had never been very lucky at games of pure chance and tonight was no exception. After barely four tries, he was getting beaten like a dusty carpet and was one loss away from having to buy more chips. Fortunately, he wasn't an adventurous gambler and only wagered an amount he could live with losing. The point was to have a good time with his friend.

Logan, on the other hand, was an entirely different animal. He wagered with all the reckless dynamism of a NASCAR driver and so far, it was working. Logan was up $500 and Tony was $250 down.

Tony glanced at his now empty glass. "I'm gonna go get another drink. You want one?"

Logan didn't turn his attention from the roulette wheel. "Gin and tonic," he said without looking back.

Tony stepped up to the bar, and in his peripheral vision, caught a glimpse of a faintly familiar face. He glanced over his shoulder and knew for sure. It was Bruce Balvin.

Tony slid his phone out of his pocket as nonchalantly as possible and sent a flash-quick text message to JJ. *Balvin is in the casino now.*

He watched as Balvin was escorted to what looked like a private gaming lounge sectioned off with velvet ropes and an imposing security guard. When Balvin approached the lounge, the burly doorman instantly stepped aside.

Tony felt a hand clap down hard on his shoulder, and his heart lurched as he whirled around.

"Geez," Logan said. "Relax."

Tony clutched his chest. "You about gave me a heart attack, man!"

"Loosen up, bro!" Logan laughed. "We're in Vegas."

After finishing their drinks and a disappointing roulette game for both, Tony knew this was a perfect time to suggest some food to pace themselves. "How about there?" Tony pointed to an upscale, eclectic diner at the far corner of the casino and ushered Logan in that direction.

He sent JJ another text. *I'm at the diner. Come join us.*

Minutes later, JJ, Gwen Q, and Rebecca arrived, and the five of them were seated at a rectangular table in the corner.

JJ glanced past Tony toward the casino. "He's in there?"

Tony nodded. "Yeah."

"Who's in where?" Logan asked with a boyish smile.

Tony narrowed his eyes. "Do you know what you're ordering, Logan?"

Logan nodded. "The roasted monkfish."

JJ's eyebrows rose. "Monkfish? At a diner? Nice." She picked up her menu and looked it over.

Rebecca, who was already flicking through the menu, nodded her recognition. "The menu here is fantastic. I was expecting more of a *diner* type diner."

Gwen Q nodded. "Though I'm not surprised. The food at the Neapolitan has been amazing since day one."

"Well, of course it is," Logan said with a proud smirk. "We designed the Neapolitan to be one of a kind. Off the charts in every way."

Just then, Tony noticed another man step into the casino. He was dressed in a dark, charcoal-grey, double-breasted suit and coffee-brown shoes.

Rebecca leaned forward, squinting. "Wait, is that—"

"Frank Gunn," Gwen Q said. "What's he doing here?"

"By the looks of it," Tony said, watching the man move through the crowd, "joining Bruce Balvin in the private gambling room."

JJ hissed and tapped forcefully on the table. "There are just too many coincidences here. Something is going on, and I'm going to find out what." She stood, then spotted a waiter and hesitated. "Then again, it doesn't hurt to order first."

They all laughed as the waiter, dressed like he was going to a fancy 50s-era sock hop, approached the table and gave a warm smile. "Welcome to Johnny's Diner. Can I take your order?"

JJ nodded. "I'll have the hackleback caviar, burrata with whipped feta, and the Nashville spicy chicken thighs."

The waiter smiled. "Great choice." He jotted on his notepad. "Any sides with the chicken?"

JJ touched her chin. "The Alaskan snow peas with almonds."

"Excellent." The waiter's grin widened. "Got it."

JJ rose to her feet and turned to Tony. "I'll be right back."

"I'm afraid to ask where you're going." Tony crossed his arms and tilted his head.

"To see if I can get into that room," she said, pointing at the private cardroom.

"Should I be the one to try?" Gwen Q asked. "Given your history with him?"

"No, better I do it. Balvin will recognize you, and it would be harder for you to explain why you're there. He already knows I'm here, *and* that I'm suspicious of him. If they stop me, he won't be surprised to hear I was snooping around him."

Gwen Q acknowledged the argument and sank back into her chair.

"Be right back," JJ said, and then she was off.

Tony watched JJ's exit and graceful approach to the private card lounge. After a moment, Logan let off a loud chortle and smacked Tony's shoulder, letting him know that his eyes may have been on JJ a tad longer than he realized.

"Now I see," Logan said with a knowing nod.

Tony glanced at him. "See what?"

Logan gave him a familiar, teasing smile. "Your anchor."

CHAPTER 21

JJ went straight for the door of the cardroom with an air of authority, a tactic with a good track record.

Unfortunately, this time, the bouncer stepped in front of her as she reached the door, and she bumped her head against his massive chest.

The man glanced down at her, seemingly taken aback at such a petite woman's stunt, like a female David going up against Goliath. "Sorry, private cardroom, ma'am."

"Oh," JJ said, feigning ignorance. "No problem. Can I just take a look?"

The bouncer looked at her suspiciously. "I'm afraid not."

Crap.

"Greetings," the bouncer said, looking over JJ's head to a patron approaching behind her. He pulled the rope aside. "Welcome back, sir."

JJ turned around to see a handsome man dressed in a midnight blue tuxedo with a martini in his hand. JJ started grinning the moment she saw him.

Bond007forlife.

Daniel Krug, Bond007forlife, beamed when he saw JJ standing there. "Are you in this game?"

The bouncer looked confused at their exchange.

JJ shook her head. "No, not today."

"Come on, you have to at least watch," Daniel said with a grin. "Though playing would be a whole lot more fun."

"I'd like to, but security here was just telling me I wasn't allowed in." JJ turned to the bouncer. Daniel did the same.

The bouncer puffed up his chest and stood silently.

Daniel took a step toward him. "She's with me."

The bouncer's eyes widened, and he hesitated. Then, he gave a deferential nod and stepped aside. "Yes, of course. Have a good evening, both of you."

Bond007forlife held out an elbow, and JJ took it and walked toward the door. She turned back to the bouncer and flashed a satisfied smile. "Thank you." Glancing toward the diner, she noticed Tony watching her. She gave him the thumbs up. Then Bond007forlife escorted her into the cardroom.

The room was upholstered in ultramarine blue with a ceiling illuminated by soft powder blue lights set behind a beautiful mural depicting a serene seascape. A waiter stepped forward holding a tray of champagne flutes.

"Champagne, madam?" he asked.

JJ nodded and took a glass. "Don't mind if I do."

They walked forward as the room opened into an expansive playing area. A single gaming table dominated the center of the room, surrounded by sofas and chaise lounges upholstered in the same shade of blue. Bond007forlife directed her to a three-seater sofa located on the shoulder of the gaming table. Directly opposite, Bruce Balvin sat accompanied by another man that JJ didn't recognize. Frank Gunn was nowhere to be seen.

The men and women at the table were locked in what looked to be a tense game of poker.

Bond007forlife leaned in to whisper. "There's half a million dollars on the line in this game."

JJ let out a quiet gasp. It took a tremendous amount of skill and impulse control to play poker when the stakes were that high. JJ, who could remember exactly how she had felt playing a game with a pot in the thousands, could only guess at the level of anxiety, tension, and hyperawareness hidden behind the stoic faces of the five players that sat around the table. On any other day she would have loved to spend an afternoon just watching their game, but today, she was here for another reason.

Plus, she had a hackleback caviar appetizer waiting for her.

She raised her chin and glanced in the direction of Bruce Balvin. He was looking right back at her. More like glaring. For a long moment, JJ experienced a flush of tension that may have rivaled that of the poker players. She thought she'd rather be anywhere else in the world than under Bruce Balvin's stare. Surprisingly, the man's face softened, and he gestured to the chair beside him.

She swallowed and leaned toward Bond007forlife. "I'll be right back."

She waited for the players to complete their hand and quietly made her way to the seat beside Bruce Balvin.

Without looking at her, he spoke in a low voice. "You're a long way from Jim Thorpe, Miss Kamaras."

"I could say the same for you," JJ said.

"Are you here for business or pleasure?" He gave a quiet snort of laughter. "Actually, what is it you do for business again?"

There was a collective gasp about the room as one of the poker players suffered from a devastating bluff.

JJ cleared her throat. "I work at my family's restaurant. You know that."

"Ah, yes," he said. "Though I'd heard an amusing rumor somewhere that you were starting a detective agency."

JJ didn't answer.

The losing player thumped the table as he surrendered all his chips.

Balvin turned at last to face her. "I surely hope you're here for pleasure, Miss Kamaras. Because it would be a real shame if you got yourself mixed up in the wrong sort of business."

JJ summoned her courage. "And what sort of business might that be?"

Balvin flashed his gem-studded teeth and delivered a menacing smile. "My business."

The terse, cold words hit like a punch.

Something moved behind the poker table, and JJ realized that what she'd thought was a wall was actually a dark curtain. Another shiver of movement, and the curtain parted completely. A woman dressed in a chic, black dress gestured toward Balvin, beckoning him to come.

The man rolled his shoulders back and rose from the sofa.

He turned and looked down at JJ. "Nosiness might be cute in Jim Thorpe, but people here are a little less accommodating. Mind your business, Miss Kamaras."

With that, he walked past the poker table and through the dark curtain. JJ sat frozen to her chair, feeling as though she was being watched without being able to see who was doing the watching. There was no point in denying it—Bruce Balvin was creepy as they came. Officer Tyrell's words flashed across her mind. *Take your small town, Agatha Christie nonsense and go home.* Her heart was beating in her chest, and a wave of doubt came over her. A small voice in the back of her head piped up. *Are you sure you should get involved in this?*

JJ and her friends had run close to danger more than once in trying to solve crimes. Perhaps it was true—men like Bruce Balvin were out of their league and above their pay grade. With her attention perched on Balvin, she was deaf to the voice behind her.

Someone touched her shoulder.

She jumped with a start.

"JJ."

It was Bond007forlife.

She shook her head and let out a breath. "What?"

He gave her a confused look. "The game's over."

"Oh, okay."

"Do you want to watch the next one?"

She glanced over at the curtain, then shook her head. "You know, I need to get back to my friends. But thanks."

Bond007forlife hesitated and gave her a worried look. "How about I come with you?"

They left the private cardroom and returned to the diner, where JJ's hackleback caviar had just arrived.

"Just in time," Gwen Q said with a smile.

Tony locked eyes with Bond007forlife, and the two exchanged a strange look that JJ was too dazed to decipher. The men had met once before, in Italy, but today they looked at each other as if they were complete strangers.

"Do you mind if I join you?" Bond007forlife asked with a smile.

"Of course we don't mind, Daniel," Rebecca said, motioning for him to sit down.

Logan, less than fully sober, extended a hand to greet Bond007forlife. "Logue the Rogue."

Bond007forlife seemed amused by the name. "Daniel Krug," he replied, shaking Logan's hand.

Gwen Q was the first to shift back into business. "What happened in there?"

JJ reclaimed her seat. "I spoke to Bruce Balvin."

"Creepy, wasn't he," Gwen Q said.

"*Oh yeah*. He told me to stay out of his business."

"What business?" Rebecca asked.

JJ shook her head. "He didn't say. He knows we started a detective agency and . . ." She hesitated. "He basically threatened me."

Bond007forlife gave a start. "Could someone fill me in with what's happening here?"

Tony sat back in his chair with his arms crossed, looking at Daniel.

Rebecca gave JJ a subtle look, and she nodded, indicating it was all right to tell him.

"We're investigating the statue that was stolen last week."

Bond007forlife raised an eyebrow. "And you think Balvin was involved?"

JJ leaned forward. "Potentially."

"Actually, he's been at all the casinos. He knows a lot of shady people." Bond007forlife hesitated a moment. "He's a platinum member at the Golden Penny casino, which is owned by the shadiest of them all—Frank Gunn. But Balvin never gambles, only watches."

Tony's phone buzzed, and when he glanced down at the caller ID, he rose to his feet and started walking away from the table. "Excuse me, I have to take this."

Bond007forlife watched Tony leave and turned back toward the table.

JJ's caviar was a gateway to heaven. One bite and she wished she could forget everything and just taste every single thing on their menu. "This caviar is incredible."

Just then, Tony returned from his call wearing a satisfied smile.

Logan stared at him. "What is it?"

"I just spoke to your brother, Victor." He turned to JJ. "We have the police reports."

CHAPTER 22

Rebecca could feel the pressure on her as they waited for her computer to finish uploading the information. The hotel room was spacious, but with five other people there staring at the back of her head, it felt tiny.

"Just a moment," Rebecca said, as she clicked once and a scanned copy of the autopsy report appeared on the screen.

She scrolled down slowly, giving everyone a chance to read.

Daniel Krug gave a disbelieving gasp as he realized what they were looking at. "You are one amazing woman, JJ. I knew you were a crackerjack poker player, but my goodness, you're a whole lot more than that."

Tony made a sound that was somewhere between a groan and a hiss.

Snoring sounded behind them, and they all glanced back. Logue the Rogue had fallen asleep on the sofa.

"Knew that was coming," Tony said with a laugh.

"Logue isn't quite the rogue he used to be," Rebecca said, smirking.

"A lot of years since he first got that name. It's about time he retired it," Tony said.

As though to confirm his agreement, Logan let off another loud snore. They all laughed before turning back to the screen.

On the page labeled summary and conclusion, Rebecca brought the scrolling to a stop. Her eyes raced across the screen, settling on the words. *Cause of death: respiratory arrest secondary to pentobarbital poisoning.*

Gwen Q's eyes widened. "Pentobarbital poisoning?"

JJ nodded. "Pentobarbital is a sedative that's lethal in large amounts. It's used to administer the death penalty."

Rebecca blinked in surprise. "How do you know that?"

"The Tara Vardanyan case," JJ replied, referring to their first murder investigation in Jim Thorpe, where JJ's brother Jason was a prime suspect. "When we were looking into causes of death, I got lost in a Wikipedia loop about lethal and poisonous drugs. I remember reading about pentobarbital and its use in death penalty cases."

Rebecca grinned and raised a fist in the air. "Sherlock is back!" She put her hand on JJ's shoulder. "I thought we lost you for a bit there."

"Elementary, my dear Watson," JJ said.

"You're supposed to say that *before* you explain, not after you . . ." Rebecca rolled her eyes. "You know what, never mind."

"So, she was poisoned," Gwen Q said.

"It appears," JJ said, raising an eyebrow.

"That means someone could have poisoned her food or a drink earlier, even the day before, right?" Gwen Q asked. "Anyone in contact with her before she died could have been responsible."

JJ shook her head. "Not with pentobarbital. It works extremely fast. That's why it's used for the death penalty—quick and painless. It had to have been administered to Winona just a moment before she died."

Rebecca tapped nervously at her keyboard, then looked up at JJ.

"What?" JJ asked.

"You saw Winona moments before her death." Rebecca shot her a sheepish look.

JJ put her hands on her hips. "Yeah, I know." She sighed. "Seems Tyrell's not the only one who loves to remind me of it."

"But this is bad, JJ," Gwen Q said, putting her head in her hands.

JJ shrugged and started to pace. "We have to track down the person who has the Arapaho and prove they were responsible for Winona's death."

"Oh, that's all?" Tony said with a smirk. "You make it sound so easy."

"It won't be easy," Rebecca said, giving JJ a confident nod and a smile. "It never is."

"The auction is our biggest chance of finding out who has the Arapaho," Gwen added.

"I agree," Rebecca said.

Gwen Q nodded. "Okay, so now what's the plan?"

"So, I've been thinking about that." Logan stood behind them. "I've got a plan."

There was silence for a long moment, then Rebecca threw back her head and let out a long, sputtering laugh. "Really Logan? What's your plan?"

The group joined Rebecca in a moment of levity.

Logan did not blink. "I am entirely serious."

JJ stopped pacing and glanced over at him. "You've been sleeping half the time we've been talking about it."

Logan smiled. "The best ideas come from dreams."

"What are you thinking, Logan?" Tony asked with a serious expression.

"We're trying to get into this auction without invitations, right?"

Gwen Q nodded. "That's right. I don't think Luke the Stickman will be willing to extend invitations to all of us."

Logan held up a finger like a professor positing a new theory. "So, you have this high-end, ultra-private gathering of people who have more money than sense. You can't step into that environment unless you're one of them."

"You're not helping," Rebecca said.

He raised a hand. "Every party has people that were never invited and yet the party can't go on without them."

"Who?" Gwen asked.

JJ smiled knowingly. "Waiters."

Tony made a low groan and looked away, his face looking grim. Something was plainly bothering him.

Logan grinned. "They are going to be hiring waiters and waitresses for this service, except they can't hire just *any* waiters from just any agency. For an event like that, I imagine you would require a high-end service from an agency that specializes in discretion. They don't want anyone at all to know about this auction. One waiter takes a picture and people could go to jail for life. You need a very talented agent to procure waiters who understand this."

JJ nodded. "He's right."

"Right about what?" Rebecca asked, "I still don't get it."

"There can't be very many agents who know where to find criminally-acquainted waiters and hosts. I don't imagine, even in Vegas, that it's a very competitive industry."

"So, we need to find the person who supplies waiters and waitresses to mobsters in Vegas?" Rebecca asked.

"Exactly," Logan said, smiling proudly. "And we may happen to know someone who knows someone in that particular line of business. Don't we, Tone?"

They all turned to face Tony who stood silently with a flat expression.

"What is he talking about?" JJ asked.

"And you think this mystery person is getting waiters for the secret auction?" Rebecca looked intrigued.

Logan nodded. "I would bet good money on it."

Tony's nostrils flared as he drew a raspy breath, and turned to JJ. "Do you remember the uncle I told you about?"

JJ blinked. "The underboss? The Cipriani guy?"

Tony nodded. "Yeah."

"Underboss?" Daniel Krug whispered.

Tony scowled at him. "My uncle used to own this pizza place with his friend Carmine."

"Pie Palace," Logan added.

Tony winced. "Started in Jim Thorpe and did pretty well. They came out here, and my uncle went big in one direction, and Carmine made a chain of the restaurant." He lowered his gaze. "In Vegas, with my uncle's connections, Carmine got involved in stuff way beyond pizza. Catering the bosses' parties, weddings. Had this running joke that the mob made the best pizza in America."

"His pizza was . . ." Logan kissed his fingers and made a loud smooching sound.

"What happened to him?" Rebecca asked. "And how does he help us?"

"He got shut down eventually," Tony explained. "Money laundering or something like that. Pie Palace doesn't exist anymore, but he still does one-off catering gigs and events like that. Has his loyal staff."

"Here in Vegas?" JJ asked.

Tony nodded. "Yeah."

"You think Carmine will know who's providing the waiters for this event?"

Tony hesitated and shrugged. "It's pretty likely."

Rebecca looked at Tony's pained face. "But are you comfortable talking to Carmine?"

Tony straightened and closed his eyes for a long moment. "I can talk to him."

JJ could see that he'd be truly going out on a limb by talking to this man. She met his eyes. "Thank you."

He blinked and nodded, then turned back to Logan. "So, we find who provides the waiters, what next?"

Logan's lips curled into a knowing smile, and he rubbed his hands together.

Gwen Q shook her head in disbelief. "Oh, no."

"Oh, yes," Logan said.

Rebecca covered her mouth. *"The Adventure of Charles Augustus Milverton."*

Tony glanced at her. "What?"

"It's one of Sherlock Holmes' short story adventures. He's working for the Lady Eva Blackwell who's being blackmailed and has to disguise himself as a plumber to get into the home of her blackmailer — Charles Milverton. This is our Milverton moment."

"I'm no use with a waiter disguise," JJ said, "Balvin knows what I look like."

"Me too," Bond007forlife added.

"I can get in with Luke the Stickman," Gwen Q said.

Tony sighed. "Carmine won't let me go in as a waiter. I'm sure of it."

Logan turned his grin to Rebecca and let out a howl. "Looks like you're rolling with Logue the Rogue, baby!"

CHAPTER 23

The dice came up with twin sixes. An odd coincidence, JJ thought, since their investigative trio had somehow grown to six. Tonight, JJ was frozen out. The only thing she could do was watch from the sideline. She had become too recognizable to join in on what was sure to be an audacious attempt at real espionage.

Tony had spoken to Carmine. It turned out the man was the boss of all bosses when it came to human resources in the Las Vegas criminal underworld. Not only did he supply wait staff for their events, but also lounge singers, dancers, musicians, caterers, cake makers, and sound technicians. A ten-minute conversation was all it took for Logan and Rebecca to be assigned part-time waiter gigs. The only requirement he gave Tony was to "make sure they obey the rules."

While Logan, Rebecca, and Gwen Q waited to receive the text message on the burner phone from Luke the Stickman for the secret event, JJ focused on finding out about the mysterious person listed in Balvin's phone as Rocky Neapolitan. She had gone through the staff list twice already, and no Rocky. *Who is this guy? And what's his connection to the Neapolitan?*

She threw the dice again and this time it came up with a two and a five. She smiled as she snatched the dice up from the velvet table. This was not a table for real gambling. It was there only as an aesthetic prop for those waiting in Montell Cooper's reception area.

"Mr. Cooper will see you now," a voice said.

She glanced up and came face-to-face with Simone, the stunning hospitality coordinator.

JJ rose from the waiting room sofa, throwing the dice back onto the velvet craps table. "Thanks, Simone."

She gave a broad smile. "You're welcome."

JJ nudged the door open and stepped inside the elegant office where Montell Cooper stood with his back to her, wrists clasped behind himself. He was staring at a large painting featuring a stern-faced man with a cigarette drooping from his mouth. Hanging just to the side of it was a large ornamental sword with a painted gold handle.

"Such a shame I am going to have to let her go soon," he said without looking back.

JJ glanced at the dark brown sofa just ahead. "Who, Simone?"

Montell glanced over his shoulder. "Of course not. I could barely count to twenty without Simone. I meant her," he said, pointing to the painting. "Any idea who painted this, Miss Kamaras?"

JJ shook her head. "None whatsoever."

He turned toward her. "A man named Galileo Lopez. A painter from Nevada who rose from abject poverty to the highest acclaim in the art world. This was one of his last paintings."

"How much is it worth?" JJ asked.

Montell tilted his head as though to size it up. "Hard to say for sure, but by now, easily several million dollars." He gestured for her to sit.

"Nice," JJ said, moving toward the sofa.

"It was Winona's doing to have the hotel buy it years ago. She wanted to showcase his work, not only as an inspiration due to his humble beginnings but also to further immerse the entire hotel in beauty. The only way she'd ever part with any of the pieces was if their proceeds were donated to a worthy charity."

"And you're thinking of doing that?"

Montell moved over to a mini refrigerator and pulled it open. "Doing what?"

"You just said how it's a shame to have to let this one go," JJ said, pointing to the Galileo Lopez painting.

"Oh, yes. I was considering it. It would represent Winona's final generous gift to the community before she . . ." The words seemed to get caught in his throat. "Would you like something to drink?"

JJ shook her head. "No, I'm fine. Thank you."

He shrugged, pulled out a bottle of sparkling water for himself, and slid into the high-backed leather desk chair directly opposite JJ, interlocking his fingers. "How can I help you, Miss Kamaras?"

JJ narrowed her eyes. "I was wondering if you knew anything about a person named Rocky?"

Montell's face gave no hint of recognition. "Rocky who?"

"That's the only name I have. One of the people we're investigating in connection with the robbery received a text message from a contact named 'Rocky Neapolitan.'"

"Really? I'm not sure I know a . . ." He let out a faint gasp. "Actually, I think we do have a Rocky." He walked over to his desk and pressed the intercom. "Simone, dear, check please if there is anyone by the name of Rocky who works with the hotel."

JJ could hear Simone clattering on a keyboard.

"There's Rocky in maintenance," she said.

"Hmm, good to know," JJ said.

There was silence for a brief moment before Simone continued. "But apparently, he just quit."

"Quit? When?" JJ asked.

There was another flurry of typing. "Looks like a few days ago. The day Miss Dakota . . ."

Montell's eyes widened as he leaned toward JJ. "You think he may be involved?"

"Not sure, but that's certainly coincidental timing," she said, staring at the ceiling with her arms crossed, deep in thought. After a moment, she asked into the intercom, "Anything else on him, Simone? A photograph at least?"

"He would have had a staff ID card," Simone said. "I can get a copy from our database and forward it to you."

"Great. And I'd love to take a look at anything else that may seem remotely connected. Any suspicious inventory, maybe purchasing orders from around the time Winona died." JJ rose to her feet.

"Where are you going?" Montell asked as JJ turned to leave his office.

"Thanks for your time, Mr. Cooper. I know you're busy, so I can just work with Simone on this administrative part and not keep bugging you."

Montell opened his mouth to speak, then seemed to think better of it. "All right."

She left the office and approached the oak reception desk just outside the office door. "Here's my cell number, Simone. You can text me the picture when you have it. Thanks again." JJ turned toward the corridor.

"No worries, will do. Is there anything else?"

"Simone, could you come into the office for a moment?" Montell called through the open door.

"I'll be in touch, Miss Kamaras," Simone said as she rose from her desk.

JJ headed for the hallway but then turned back. Something felt off. She hesitated for a moment, her mind racing, then took a step back toward the reception desk. She could hear the hushed tones of Simone and Montell in the office through the crack in the door. JJ took another quiet step, and now behind the desk, she glanced at Simone's computer screen where several windows were open. One page appeared to be an employee list. Another was a document on business letterhead from the Nevada Food Bank Charitable Trust. Yet another was a bank statement. JJ looked more closely at the statement and noted some unusual entries. A charge from a chemical company, and in parentheses, what looked like some sort of chemical equation. She looked further down the list.

JJ did a double take.

Her eyes were glued to an entry at the bottom of the page—a payment to Executive Services, Inc. for fifty thousand dollars. JJ stepped quickly away from the desk as she tried to piece together these seemingly disparate bits of information. She needed to find space to think. Clear her mind.

Ah, an idea.

Simone looked surprised to see JJ still standing in the reception area. She slipped into her desk chair. "Did you need something else, Miss Kamaras?"

"Actually, yes. Sorry to bother you again, but I do have one more request. It might sound a little strange."

Simone looked up at her. "No problem, what is it?"

"I'd like to spend some time in one of the hotel's kitchens. If it's not too much trouble, that is. Not cooking for guests or anything. Maybe just a corner of the kitchen to create a dish for myself. I just need to be cooking. It helps me think."

Simone sat back, looking surprised. "Sure, I suppose so."

JJ nodded. "My family owns a restaurant. There's something about being in a kitchen that just reminds me of home. Helps me to focus my mind."

Simone squinted at JJ. "I see, yes, certainly. Please feel free to go into Ishin or any of the kitchens in any of our restaurants." She pulled a business card from her inner pocket. "Give them this, and tell them I said you should be allowed into the kitchen. Any issues, have them call me."

JJ took the card and smiled. "Thank you."

* * *

Minutes later, JJ found herself in the kitchen of the Japanese steakhouse Ishin, which was fairly quiet as the restaurant was still a few hours away from opening. She felt the countertops that were cut from light pinewood. Wooden frame cupboards were above them. She made her way to a small butcher block style island off to the side and away from the main work area of the kitchen, her eyes grazing the suspended racks of spices and cutlery.

"What should I cook?" she wondered aloud, as she pulled a crisp, white chef's uniform from the folded stack and slipped a hand into one of the sleeves. She felt better already.

Pulling open a refrigerated drawer, she found fresh-picked vegetables of every kind, from broccoli to Yamashita spinach. There were thick cuts of lamb, beef, and pork arranged next to lobster and salmon on ice. She felt her mind wandering as it found its way home.

She took out the ingredients she needed and set up her station under the bright light of the island. She started with the potatoes, peeling them the way her father had taught her when she was a little girl.

It was barely five minutes before she'd become lost in the work. The world around her faded. The rhythmic thud of the knife as she minced spring onions seemed to dance with the beating of her heart. Under the light, she felt a light sweat start to build under her chef's whites. In that moment of flow and focus, she felt the beginnings of clarity—just like always.

What are the puzzle pieces?

She whispered aloud to herself. "The air conditioning. Balvin and Gunn. The auction. Rocky Neapolitan. $50k for unknown executive services. A charge for chemicals. The Nevada Food Bank Charitable Trust..."

JJ continued to cook in total silence. She folded the vegetables, flattening them over one another into a kaleidoscope of flavor.

Unconnected parts that had once seemed coincidental started to meld together like the sweet does with the sour. She smiled as she tossed hand-washed grains of rice into a simmering pan of water. What she was cooking was an audacious creation—a Greek and Japanese fusion that just had to be an original. Spanakopita bao buns, black rice, wagyu beef gyros, and sushi drizzled with creamy tzatziki with just a hint of wasabi.

She set a place at the counter and sat down to eat, savoring each bite.

There were things she had to do. But for now, she was content to eat alone in silence, trusting that everything was falling into place.

Her phone vibrated in her pocket—a text from Gwen Q. "The auction is tonight. We're on."

CHAPTER 24

⁕

Rebecca tugged at the cuffs of her ill-fitting tuxedo shirt. They had spent hours in what looked like an old rec center with an irritable man named Carl who taught them the ins and outs of being a waiter at the event.

"This is a highly private and exclusive night. No phones, no pictures, no idle conversation, no flirting, no names, no second looks. Your job is to take orders and serve food courteously. If I get one complaint—true or untrue—you're done. And I hope you understand that means a whole lot more than you're fired."

Rebecca swallowed hard. While she stifled a feeling of panic, Logan seemed to revel in the entire affair. Gwen Q had received the text from Luke the Stickman, but the wait staff had not been informed of any details. They were going in blind, which really put Rebecca on edge. *What if people have guns there?*

"The bus is outside waiting," Carl announced. "We leave in five minutes."

The dozen or so men and women in tuxedo uniforms filed out of the room and spilled out into the parking lot where a gray minivan was waiting with the door already open.

A hulking bald man who looked like an angry Mr. Clean stood outside the door holding a basket. "Your phone."

Rebecca glanced into the basket and saw the collection of phones from all of the other wait staff. Turning the phone off, she placed it inside. A second phone was strapped to her ankle and tucked into her sock. All she had to hope for now was a less than thorough search. She felt sure Logan had a second phone hidden somewhere as well.

After dropping their phones, Rebecca and Logan climbed into the minivan. Logan was still smiling as though he knew something that no one else did. She wondered if he looked suspicious to anyone else and wanted to tell him to stop grinning, but it seemed impossible now to speak privately to him with all of them seated so close together.

"Any idea where we're going this time?" a man asked from behind her.

Rebecca glanced over her shoulder and saw a plump man with a nose that looked like it had been broken at least once. He smiled when their eyes met and gave a bashful look. "Just asking."

Rebecca gave a polite smile but offered no spoken response.

The windows to the minivan were covered in white paint, making it impossible to see into or out of it.

Within five minutes, on perfect cue, the engine roared to life. The doors slid shut and the minivan took off down the street. In totality, the trip must have taken twenty-five minutes and included areas of rough, bumpy road that reminded Rebecca of the trips to her great aunt's farm in Ireland, where the road was more dirt than asphalt.

They came at last to a stop and the door was pulled open, pouring light into the van. Just ahead was the service entrance of what looked like a large factory warehouse.

"Let's move," Carl growled.

He led from the front as they were ushered in through a large cargo door. It took a moment for them to realize exactly what this structure was.

"Incredible," Logan said, staring up at the ceiling. "It's an old airplane hangar."

Rebecca blinked and nodded. "Yup."

It was decorated in a festive manner but was still an airplane hangar, just dressed up for a grand dinner.

Rebecca instinctively reached for her phone before realizing it was strapped to her ankle and only to be used for dire emergencies and away from viewing eyes.

"Quick search," Carl announced, indicating where they were to form a line. A broad-shouldered man with dark hair and wearing a face mask approached from the distance. He was plainly in charge of security.

Search? Rebecca's heart started to paddle against her chest.

Logan, who she was now convinced had been drinking, still smiled even at the invitation to a search.

Rebecca kept her eyes fixed on the ground as she inched forward with the line to get searched.

"Next," Carl hissed impatiently, as it came to her turn.

Her eyes watching the floor, she stepped forward. The masked man began his search. She felt his grip on her wrist as he trailed down her sleeves. He patted down her front and back, then started on her legs. In a final move, he reached for the ankle where her phone was strapped.

She held her breath as the man's hand closed around the sock and quite obviously gripped the phone. She winced. *This is it. What if they kill me?*

The security guard hesitated and stood up slowly.

Rebecca stood frozen.

"All clear, go ahead."

Her heart nearly exploded at those words. *All clear? How?*

She glanced up at the security guard and for the first time caught a proper glimpse at him. He pulled his mask down slightly and winked, quickly returning to his stoic expression.

It was Max, JJ's ex from the casino in Jim Thorpe.

A man who had broken JJ's heart.

A friend once.

Part of Rebecca wished she could poke a finger in his chest and berate him for what happened with JJ and for leaving Jim Thorpe so suddenly. Clearly, that was a tongue-lashing meant for another time. Relief flooded over her as she realized there would be no cry of alarm. She had an ally. Kind of.

She nodded to Max and moved past him a few paces before realizing that Logan was right behind her. Max didn't know Logan, and if he found a phone on him, no way he'd let it slide. She turned back, trying to catch Max's eye, but it was no hope. Carl was watching everything like a hawk. Max was going to search Logan and there was nothing she could do to stop it.

She watched with a mounting feeling of dread as Max searched. Thoroughly. It seemed an eternity. Rebecca was sure their cover was blown.

Max stood up and inhaled deeply. Then waved Logan on through.

"Don't you have your phone?" she whispered, as Logan stepped up beside her.

He nodded. "Yeah."

She raised an eyebrow and whispered. "Where?"

He grinned and pointed to his belt.

Rebecca shot him a confused look. "It's a belt."

"Not just any belt. A Vegas money belt."

Rebecca sized up his belt from several angles as they moved forward in the line, trying not to draw attention. "How is there a phone in it?"

"Ah, Logue the Rogue is more clever than you think."

"Talking about yourself in the third person is more weird than you think."

"The ultra micro mini—smallest smartphone made to date. Just got it," he whispered, still smiling. "Two inches long, razor thin, and fits in the belt's secret inside zipper."

Rebecca gave a quiet laugh and shook her head. She'd heard of the ultra micro mini in her tech travels, but leave it to Logue the Rogue to wait to test it out during the height of espionage.

They spread out across the hangar and began setting the tables and preparing a small stage with a wooden podium for the event. After ninety minutes or so, the first guests started to appear, and

Carl ordered the wait staff to quickly serve the champagne and canapés.

"Remember people, no names, no second looks, capiche? Go!"

Rebecca had not come for names and looks. It was only because JJ couldn't be there, and sometimes, Watson had to step in for Sherlock for the good of the case. She studied the room, looking out for something, anything, that could lead them to the Arapaho and the people responsible for Winona Dakota's death.

In three quick trips around the banquet area, she had depleted her tray of champagne and taken inventory of everyone who might be important. On her fifth trip, she saw Gwen Q arrive alongside a long-haired, tattooed man whom she recognized as Luke the Stickman. They locked eyes and each gave the other a slight nod.

Rebecca moved past a huddle of three men speaking in low tones. Two wore dark suits without ties and the third wore a subtle, bone-white collared shirt with gaudy gold cufflinks.

The man in the cufflinks spoke in a loud and arrogant tone. "How do you think they got their hands on it?"

One man in a dark suit spoke up. "The people who stole it must have reached out to them."

"Or they stole it themselves," the second suited man offered.

"And killed that woman from TV?" the man in cufflinks asked.

Dark suit number one shrugged. "Accidents happen."

Cupping his chin in thought, the man's cufflinks caught the light overhead and flashed in Rebecca's eyes. "I don't think they stole it. They're working for someone."

"Who?" the dark-suited men asked in unison.

The cufflinked man glanced over his shoulder suspiciously and came face to face with Rebecca.

Her heart lurched and her champagne try wobbled as she looked back at him. "Champagne?"

He frowned and shook his head. The others did the same.

Rebecca wanted desperately to listen to the vital end of that conversation. They waited for her to leave before they resumed.

As she walked away, she strained to hear but caught only the ghost of words. She was so immersed in her attempt to eavesdrop that she almost missed Bruce Balvin's entrance into the crowd. He looked like a wise guy out of a classic casino heist movie—tan suit, brown cravat, and a fat cigar in his mouth. His eyes brushed over in her direction and bore no hint of recognition, but there were also many people between them. She couldn't get closer without looking obvious.

Gwen Q, however, had no such restriction. She glided over to him and struck up a conversation as smoothly as one would scratch a match to a fire.

Rebecca smiled as she turned toward the other side of the room. The man with the cufflinks was arguing now with the men in dark suits as they strode toward the dinner tables.

"I'm telling you. It's definitely that dude from back east. Why else would he come here dressed like Sam Rothstein from *Casino*? He thinks he's got a hundred mill coming his way."

Rebecca became still and tried to listen as nonchalantly as possible as the men walked past. They had to be talking about Bruce Balvin. He was, after all, dressed like a mafia money man. The hundred million. Did that mean the Arapaho? Is that what it would go for at one of these things?

She turned toward the kitchen to get a fresh tray of champagne glasses and saw Max standing just off to the side. She arched her path to walk toward him and they moved together toward the kitchen.

"What are you doing here?" she asked.

"I should ask you that. I'm working. What's your excuse?"

"Also working," Rebecca said.

Max looked confused, then let out a humorless chuckle. "Don't tell me. You're with JJ, investigating the Arapaho, aren't you?"

Rebecca didn't answer.

"Listen, if you are, you won't find it here. Not tonight anyway."

Rebecca glanced up at him, still walking toward the kitchen. "What do you mean?"

"They brought it here. But there was a fire at one of the buffet tables about ten minutes ago, and it must have spooked them. They took it away. It's no longer for sale tonight."

Rebecca pushed the kitchen door open, and Max followed her inside. "Where are they keeping it?"

Max shook his head. "I don't know exactly. I'm sure some vault somewhere with twenty-four-hour security and surveillance."

"You mean, like a bank?" she asked.

A familiar voice sounded behind her. "In Vegas, no one keeps their valuables in the bank." Logan held a half-empty bottle of champagne. "Bet you anything, I know where they're keeping it."

CHAPTER 25

The next morning, JJ, Tony, and Logan sat waiting for the others to join them.

The waiter grinned as he dropped a fat stack of pancakes at the center of their table. A small rectangle of butter melted slowly at the top.

JJ's wide eyes took in the sight. "Looks good."

Tony nodded in agreement across from her. "Yup."

"Enjoy," the waiter said. "It's unlimited pancakes until noon."

He dropped the maple syrup off and turned back toward the kitchen.

JJ glanced at her watch. It was two minutes past nine. The rest were supposed to be here already.

The door opened. It was Rabbit, all smiles.

Logan jumped up to greet him. "Rabbit, my man! You're back in action!" Then he sat back down and rubbed the side of his head. "Whoa, do I need an aspirin."

They all started on the pancakes and looked up when the restaurant door swung open. Rebecca stepped inside with Gwen Q. A third person walked in after them—tall, handsome, with shoulders like a bridge.

JJ winced. *Max.*

When she'd heard they saw him at the secret auction, she was unsure how to react to the news. It would be a lie to say she hadn't missed him when he left Jim Thorpe. And she knew there was a possibility she'd bump into him, but to see him now brought up a mix of emotions.

The three joined their table and the waiter soon reappeared.

"It's twenty dollars for all you can eat pancakes until noon," the waiter explained.

Tony raised his fork with a poked-through piece of pancake and nodded his approval. "It's good."

"I'll get the pancakes," Rebecca said.

"Me, too," Gwen Q added.

Max locked eyes with JJ. "I'm fine."

To her relief and surprise, she felt no anxiety in seeing Max. Her heart felt still, and her mind felt at ease. "Thanks for coming, Max. It's good to see you."

He smiled. "Likewise. And I'm happy to help however I can."

Gwen Q lowered her chin. "It looks like we know where the Arapaho is."

"What?" JJ's eyes grew wide. "How?"

Rebecca gestured to Logan who wasted no time in saying his piece.

"I figured that if the Arapaho was still in Vegas, it could only be in one of a few places. The very best casinos in Las Vegas have the finest safe rooms money can buy. I remember when we were designing the Neapolitan. The vault at the center of the building cost more than most single floors."

"Wow," JJ said.

Logan nodded. "I figured, if we ruled out the Neapolitan, it would go to the next big competitor close by. One perhaps with a questionable reputation."

"The Golden Penny?" JJ asked.

"That's right." Logan said, "So imagine my delight when I saw one of my brother Victor's good pals from the police department who's now the head of security at the Golden Penny. He was undercover at our little secret auction yesterday, scoping the place out."

"I'm still not seeing how you know the Arapaho is at the Golden Penny," Tony said.

Logan grinned. "Because I knew if they were there to sell the Arapaho that night, they would panic at even the slightest glitch in their plans. Get the sculpture out of there at the faintest hint of a problem and high-tail it to the nearest safe space. A safe space, I should add, that wouldn't balk at harboring a priceless stolen artifact."

"What are you saying?" Max's face showed his surprise. "You staged the disturbance? You spooked them?"

Logan's face broke into a wide cat-that-ate-the-canary grin. "Maybe."

"What did you do?" Tony insisted, in an almost parental tone.

"Oh, just a little mishap where I knocked over the burner under one of the chafing dishes."

"You set that table on fire?" Max's eyes grew wide.

"I plead the fifth," he said and then let out a howl of a laugh. "They freaked out, just as I thought they would, and two enormous thugs raced the Arapaho out of there. But I was watching the exits. I saw the armored vehicle that sped off and knew the sculpture was in it, so I took down the license plate. Turns out it belongs to a security company called Gold Security Services which is managed by a parent company, FG Enterprises, which is owned by—"

"Frank Gunn," JJ finished.

Logan nodded. "That's right. Owner of the Golden Penny."

JJ snapped her fingers. "I knew it."

Max leaned forward. "Knew what?"

"Frank Gunn and Bruce Balvin. They're the ones responsible for the robbery and Winona Dakota's death. They had to have an insider at the Neapolitan, presumably this Rocky guy. If that's even his real name." JJ was deep in thought for a moment.

"What?" Gwen Q asked.

"I don't know," JJ said. "Other things that I noticed. Weird things I saw on Simone's computer."

"You broke into her computer?" Gwen asked as Rebecca enthusiastically gave her a thumbs up.

"No, she had left her desk for a minute, so I just happened to glance over..."

"Nice! What did you see?"

"One was a purchasing order that had some kind of chemical name."

Rabbit perked up. "What kind of chemical?"

"Rabbit used to be the chemistry king," Logan explained to the group. "Before he killed most of his brain cells."

"I don't know. It was like an equation, with C's and H's," JJ said. "CHCl something, like with a number two. Or three maybe?"

"Ah, three chicklets," Rabbit said with authority. "That's how we used to remember it."

"Remember what?" Tony asked, looking irritated. "No more games, please, Rabbit."

"It's not a game! Chicklet was the mnemonic device—like a memory system—we used in organic chemistry. To remember the chemical formula $CHCl_3$."

"C-H... whatever. How is this helping?" Tony asked impatiently. "What does it stand for?"

"It's chloroform." Rabbit sat back and folded his arms across his chest.

JJ's eyes were as big as saucers. "Rabbit, you're a genius!"

"Yeah, I get that a lot," he said with a wide grin, as Tony and Logan rolled their eyes.

"And why, oh, why would a hotel need chloroform unless they intended to subdue someone?" JJ asked. "Rabbit, does it have any odor?"

"Yes, kind of like a sweet, chemical smell. Sort of like chlorine, but not exactly."

JJ recalled being in Winona's room that day. It smelled like cleaning chemicals, not too different from what she noticed at the Lexington Motel. But unlike the motel, in Winona's room, she'd started to feel woozy after being in there just a few minutes. "And there were other things I saw on Simone's computer, too. An official letter to a charity, the Nevada Food Bank Charitable Trust."

"That's not so weird. Winona liked charities," Gwen Q said.

"Right, but when I googled it, nothing concrete came up." JJ looked at Rebecca. "Could you—"

"On it, Sherlock." Rebecca jotted down the name on a paper napkin and put it in her pocket.

"Then, get this, a charge for fifty thousand dollars for 'executive services,'" JJ added.

"What!" Gwen Q scowled. "Sounds *way* shady."

"It sure does," Tony agreed. "But can we prove all this? Chloroform? Gunn and Balvin's involvement?"

"Not yet. But the pieces are lining up and starting to tell us their story. I think, we find the Arapaho, the rest unravels," JJ said with confidence.

Tony looked unconvinced. "But it's probably locked up in some safe somewhere behind twenty inches of steel."

"So, right, a few legitimate obstacles," JJ agreed, waving her hand dismissively. "But we need to find it. Okay, ideas, people. Come on."

Rebecca's eyes grew wide, and she snapped her head toward JJ and grinned. "*The Red-Headed League.*"

"What?" JJ asked. She hesitated, then gasped. "You're not serious."

"As a heart attack." Rebecca smiled deviously.

JJ shook her head, but slowly a smile grew on her face. "You're crazy, Rebecca Brannigan. Certifiable."

Gwen Q looked back and forth at both of them, twice. "Oh, no. No, you're *both* crazy."

"What are we crazy about?" Tony asked, confused.

"*The Red-Handed League* is a Sherlock Holmes story," JJ explained.

Tony slapped his forehead. "Again, with the Sherlock. What's this one about?"

Rebecca grinned. "A bank heist."

"*Yes!*" Logan thumped the table. "Now we're talking!"

Tony raised his hands. "Wait, wait, wait, what do you mean here? Stealing from a casino?"

"Not stealing. You can't steal something that was stolen in the first place. We'd merely be recovering," JJ clarified.

"How do you expect us to stage a casino heist when Logan is barely able to pour syrup on his pancakes," Tony said, pointing.

"Now that hurt, buddy," Logan said, raising an offended hand to his chest.

JJ's face showed her resolve. "Gunn and Balvin are behind this. Or they are deeply involved, at the very least. We find the statue, we can prove they're responsible. The police here won't listen to a word we say."

"I don't know, JJ. Investigating is one thing." Tony shook his head. "But a heist?"

"We can't just leave, Tony!" JJ said, putting her hand on his arm. "We've come this far, and we're so close. We have to finish this. We owe Winona that. We owe ourselves that."

"I think it could be a bridge too far," Tony said.

"It probably is," JJ admitted. "But *we're* going to cross it either way," she said, gesturing to the rest of the group. "You coming?"

He gave her a long, studying look, and for a moment, JJ wondered if he was going to get up and walk out.

Then he sat up straight and gave her a nod. "I'm coming."

JJ lowered her chin and grinned. "Good, because I have a plan."

* * *

NOAH PULLED the limousine up right by the curb. Gwen Q stepped out onto the red carpet in a curve-hugging leopard print dress with six-inch gold heels. Cameras flashed, and the desperate men and women of the press aimed their lenses begging her to look *over here! over here!* assuming she was some sort of celebrity. Gwen Q flashed a smile and waved as her date for the night emerged from the limousine. A tall, dashing man in a black tuxedo with the undeniable charm of his online namesake—*Bond007forlife*.

A third man went ahead of them to clear the way and to further sell the idea that they really were a celebrity couple. Max played the part perfectly. Crowds parted like the Red Sea as they strode into the hotel. Their destination, the casino's private table. They were there to play the game of their lives.

* * *

REBECCA LET out a long breath as she stared at the panel of screens. Red dots indicated the location of her friends as they moved around the sprawling, digitally rendered blueprint of the Golden Penny. It had taken three hours to digitize it using the architectural drawings Logan retrieved from an industry connection. Another hour to set up the wires. But it would all be well worth the trouble. She just hoped and prayed that there were no surprises in the structure.

"Everyone good?" Rebecca asked.

"Good," came the whispered reply from Gwen Q.

"Good," said Tony who stood next to Logan.

Rebecca hesitated, awaiting the final confirmation. It didn't come.

"JJ?"

There was no answer.

"JJ are you there?"

The device's playback bubbled in the tense silence.

"Sherlock?"

Another long moment passed. "I'm here," she said at last. "All good."

Rebecca let out a sigh of relief. "All right then, people. Showtime."

* * *

SHOWTIME. *Easy for you to say,* JJ thought.

She looked forward and considered the task ahead of her. *Don't look down.*

'You're the only one that can make that jump,' Rebecca had said.

Now she wished she had told her to forget it. It wasn't a completely *impossible* jump, to be clear. She stood on the roof of the Golden Penny's maintenance tower, staring over at the adjacent building that housed the hotel's coveted private wing. She looked across the divide toward the exclusive suite's wide balcony—her destination. It seemed an endless expanse of air away, but she estimated only fifteen feet or so. She peeked at the ground far below and shuddered. She had to clear the balcony railing or . . . *no, don't think of that. Remember your training.* Her mother, Athena, had coached her well during her formative gymnastics years in both the physical and mental skills of a champion. How to laser focus. How to envision the stunt as already completed flawlessly. How to muster her power from her core.

Just one jump.

She bounced on the balls of her feet on the far end of the roof just like she used to do when preparing for a difficult vault. She drew in breath, pumped her arms, and took off running. With each step closer to the edge, her heart beat harder until it reached a crescendo. She poured every last ounce of might into the final step and propelled herself forward as if shot from a cannon. For a long, suspended moment, she was flying.

* * *

REBECCA'S VOICE sounded in Tony's earpiece.

"How are we looking?" she asked.

Tony glanced ahead. "So far, so good."

He was wearing a yellow neon vest that allowed him to make his way through the hotel and successfully stay under the radar.

Undeniably, the Golden Penny was a superb casino. The gambling hall was lit by a dozen twinkling crystal chandeliers, and the people shone and sparkled even more brightly than the lights. It *was* Vegas after all. Still, Tony couldn't help but think of the underside to all of the glitz and beauty and that there must be a good reason the Golden Penny always seemed to draw sideways glances when mentioned among the Strip's top hotels.

He came to the end of the gambling hall and passed by a group of waistcoated dealers. They wore perfectly crisp uniforms and were groomed with all the careful attention of champion show ponies. He walked into the posh restaurant on the gambling floor and made his way to the industrial kitchen at the rear. He almost laughed at how easy it was. The vest worked like a magic wand.

He strode past the walk-in freezer and the cast-iron oven, arriving at a grim metallic door that bore no sign. To his grateful surprise, it was slightly ajar and a firm pull was all it took to open it all the way. He stepped into a narrow corridor with a low-slung ceiling and proceeded forward.

He came at last to his destination. The sign above the door read Surveillance.

He gritted his teeth and pushed the door. He groaned aloud. It was locked. They hadn't planned for this.

He knocked twice and a face appeared in the small door window.

A bespectacled man with a scraggly red-brown beard looked at him suspiciously. "Who are you?"

Tony pointed at his vest where the words Golden Penny Maintenance were boldly written. The man in the window gave him a confused look.

"We didn't call for maintenance. You've got the wrong room."

Tony's answer could have been better. "No, sir, I was called."

"Check again," the red-bearded man said as he shook his head and walked away from the door. Tony sighed in frustration. He had to get into that room somehow. Their entire plan depended on it.

He knocked a second time and the red-bearded man appeared again with an exasperated, angry, look on his face. "What's wrong with you? Why are you still here?"

Tony tried anger this time, contorting his face into a scowl. "Because you won't let me do my job!"

The red-bearded man threw his hands up in apparent disgust, then pulled the door open.

"What is it with you?" he asked.

Tony closed the distance between them, getting almost nose to nose. "If you don't let me do my job, our entire system is going to be down, and you'll be blamed for it. Now let me in, or I'm reporting you to Mr. Gunn."

The name Gunn had worked like a charm. He straightened, suddenly alive with attention. "Fine, but make it quick. We don't have all day."

Tony gave a businesslike nod as he slipped into the room. *I'm in.* Now came the challenging part. He stared up at the panel of screens at the far end of the room. He touched the small USB storage device in his pocket, recalling Rebecca's words when the plan was made. *Tony, we need you to hack their surveillance system.*

She'd given him an in-depth tutorial just a few hours earlier. He glanced at the sophisticated computer at the far end of the room and took a deep breath. "Here goes nothing."

CHAPTER 26

JJ landed in a squat on the balcony, having cleared the railing by a hair. She looked back at the maintenance roof. Her heart was pounding so hard she felt she could hear it. She started to laugh. It was perhaps the most daring thing she had ever done, and the exhilaration was intoxicating.

She stood up and walked quickly to the balcony's sliding glass door, finding it unlocked. She inched it open, peered in to find it empty, and stepped into the luxurious suite. It was dimly lit with a bedside table lamp, the only one to illuminate the shiny dresses scattered across the unmade bed. JJ took a minute to view her surroundings, then slipped out into the corridor. She had made it to the exclusive private tower of the casino, where only the highest profile guests could afford to stay.

She walked quietly down the corridor and came to the emergency stairwell. She pushed against the heavy handlebar, unlocking the door. Stepping into the fluorescent light of the stairwell was a man with a dark handlebar mustache.

"Hi, Alex," JJ said with a smile.

He smiled back. "You made it."

They turned toward the private elevator. "Did you ever doubt me?"

Alex's eyebrows rose. "Uh, yeah."

He produced a plastic card and slid it through the wall-mounted card reader. The red light flashed green and the low thrum of an elevator sounded several floors below. A sharp ping sounded as the doors opened, and they stepped inside to go to the top floor of the hotel and its most enviable suite—the eleventh floor penthouse.

JJ touched her earpiece and spoke aloud. "Watson, we're in."

* * *

Rebecca slapped her thigh with excitement at JJ's communication. Then, when a small notification appeared at the corner of her central screen, her heart leaped in her chest again—*access granted*. She double-clicked on the notification and followed the prompts until the screen was illuminated with grayscale surveillance camera footage. Tony had done it. He had hacked the security cameras.

She cleared her throat and spoke into the microphone with the next crucial message. "Blackout in ten minutes, team. I repeat, blackout in ten minutes."

* * *

The security guard closest to Tony slapped a hand on his shoulder. "All right, let's go, buddy."

Tony snarled as he was dragged away by hotel security, yelling, "What's wrong with you? I was called to fix the problem!"

Inwardly, Tony wanted to grin but there would be time soon enough, he hoped, to revel in their victory. While security was busy wrestling him away from the mainframe, he had diverted their attention from his true goal—the in-built USB port for the surveillance system. It was such a simple plant, and yet, they had missed it completely. He felt like a magician using misdirection and sleight of hand to completely befuddle a crowd. While he plugged away noisily at the mainframe with one hand, he quietly accessed the USB port a couple feet away with the other. A simple move he'd learned by being the victim of such a trick, now put to sophisticated use. Ted Cookie had taught him well.

* * *

Gwen Q and Bond007forlife strode purposefully toward the private gaming room with Max walking just behind them. The bouncer there took one look at Max, who must have spoken a secret bouncer language, and let them through without a moment's hesitation.

They strode over to the central table, where three other men were about to begin a game of poker. Gwen Q glanced up at the dealer. He was a tall, skinny man who barely filled out his waistcoat.

"Private table," the dealer announced as they approached.

Gwen Q made a pointed effort to meet the eyes of the man who sat directly across from her. Bruce Balvin glanced down at his cards for a moment before meeting her eye. When their eyes met, he smiled briefly, then glanced at Bond007forlife and scowled, apparently realizing he was her actual date.

"So, we meet again," he said with a wry smile.

Gwen Q nodded. "Indeed, we do."

Balvin glanced toward the man to his left. The man who carried all the clout at the establishment. "Can she join us at the table?"

Frank Gunn looked Gwen Q up and down slowly in a way that made her skin crawl, then spoke in a low, guttural voice. "Sure."

He stretched the word out so it sounded like he was mocking her.

"Welcome," the dealer said, brandishing a smile.

Bond007forlife stepped forward and placed his hands on the edge of the table. "Good evening, gentlemen. This is going to be fun."

The poker game began in earnest and the two men soon learned that Bond007forlife was no novice. In just a few hands, he had punished them with bluffs and calls so brutally direct that they seemed powerless to oppose his dominance on the table. After another audacious bluff, Frank Gunn looked like he wanted to gut punch him.

Bond007forlife gave a politely apologetic smile which made Frank

Gunn sip angrily from his whiskey glass. Gwen Q glanced at her watch and noted the time, then she looked up to the dealer and gave him a subtle nod. The dealer nodded back, then touched the small gold chain on his neck that had a cookie for a pendant.

The lights went off and Frank Gunn made a sharp sound of alarm. The darkness held only briefly, but Gwen Q hoped that Ted Cookie really was as good a pickpocket as they had been led to believe. The lights were restored a moment later, but Frank Gunn now seemed irreparably paranoid.

"I am afraid we might have to cancel our game for the time being Mister..."

"Craig," Bond007forlife offered. "Daniel Craig."

In extending a hand, Daniel managed to knock off a stack of chips, sending them rolling out through the private room door.

Commotion set in as people from the surrounding tables couldn't help but stare at their table.

"Sorry," Bond007forlife said, rummaging for the chips. "I'm so clumsy."

With chaos ensuing around him, Bruce Balvin sat silently, seeming to count something in his head.

"This is unacceptable," Frank Gunn snarled. "We're better than this."

Gwen Q laughed under her breath. *You ain't seen nothing yet.*

* * *

As soon as the power was cut, JJ moved fast. She strode into the penthouse and made her way toward the large safe that the architectural map showed was behind a fish tank. Alex moved with equal speed, knocking out the main surveillance camera in the room. JJ climbed over the top of the fish tank and managed to maneuver through the small space between the tank and the ceiling with catlike agility.

When the lights came back on, they were in place and ready. They waited for the last critical piece of information—the combination to the safe.

* * *

GWEN Q and Bond007forlife waited for Frank Gunn and Bruce Balvin to leave before turning to their fake dealer, Ted Cookie.

"Did you get it?" Gwen Q asked impatiently.

"What do you think I am, an amateur?" Cookie said with a smirk, brandishing the phones he had stolen. Using the IMEI number, Gwen Q was able to unlock Frank Gunn's emergency feature to send out a message to the top brass. She typed furiously, knowing that in a moment, they'd have to scatter. She hit send. As far as Gunn's people would know, the message came from him: *'Remind me the code to the safe. I need to check something. Urgent.'*

Bond007forlife watched her work, wide-eyed. "Impressive. You belong on the big screen."

"You're smooth, Bond."

Bond007forlife almost blushed. "So, what do we do now?"

Gwen Q looked around. "We head back to the Neapolitan and pray everything else goes as planned."

Rebecca's voice sounded through their wires. "Excellent work, guys. Safe combination sent."

* * *

FRANK GUNN SLIPPED into the elevator. "Eleventh," he said, not bothering to glance at the elevator attendant in the corner. "Hurry." He hit an icon on his phone, which kept pulling up a black screen. Gunn put the phone to his ear and barked at the receiver. "The security cameras in my room are showing nothing but black. They're out! Get someone on it. Now!"

He noticed the elevator was going the wrong way. He at last turned to the porter in the corner. "I said eleventh, you dolt!"

Logan stepped into the light. "Sorry, sir, no eleventh floor today."

Gunn scowled. "What are you talking about? I said eleventh!"

Logan lunged at him hard and fast and struck Gunn with such virile force that the man was forced to his knees. "Say goodnight, sir." He struck again and Gunn fell unconscious. When the elevator came to the basement, he pulled Gunn's limp body into the doorway to jam the elevator, then raced into the corridor and up the stairs.

* * *

JJ GRASPED the large dial for a final turn. She held her breath. Then it came—a soft, satisfying click. Slowly, she pulled the heavy door aside.

There it was.

The sculpture certainly was a masterpiece.

Never intended to be sold, no matter what the price. She tucked it into her duffel bag and carefully handed it over the fish tank to Alex.

For a split second, Alex hesitated and smiled a devious grin. Had she been unwise letting him help? What if he ran with it and tried to sell it? Alex stood frozen, holding the statue.

Trust your instincts, Constanza had said. No, she knew in that moment, in her gut, she'd made the right choice.

Heck, he couldn't outrun her anyway.

With effortless flourish, she vaulted over the fish tank, and together they sprinted from the room, exploding into the emergency stairwell, jumping two steps at a time all the way down.

CHAPTER 27

JJ took a long sip from her coffee cup as she waited for Montell to call her into his office. She looked over at a polished table with a set of business cards in a shiny gold holder that she hadn't noticed before. She picked one up. *Montell Cooper, General Manager, The Neapolitan Hotel and Casino.* JJ tossed the dice onto the decorative craps table and it came up with a four and a five. *For the forty-five years they'll serve for killing Winona Dakota*

Simone set down the receiver and called out to her. "Mr. Cooper will see you now."

JJ rose to her feet and gave Simone a considering look. "Thank you."

She entered Montell's office, and he rushed to pull her into an embrace. "You did it! You found the sculpture. You're going to be a star after this. The press will just eat it up! We'll make you a lifetime ambassador for the hotel. You can be even bigger than Winona Dakota was!"

JJ didn't stir. "Is my check ready?"

Montell grinned and straightened his cream-colored ascot. "Straight to business. I love it. Yes, here it is, and I added a healthy bonus for all the great work you did." He handed over a signed check.

JJ inspected it and folded it carefully, placing it in her shirt pocket. "Thank you."

"I can't believe a man of Frank Gunn's stature was responsible. He operates a casino, for goodness sake."

"You operate a casino."

"Well, yes," Montell explained. "But ours is of the highest esteem and beyond reproach. He gives us all a bad name."

"Really." JJ stared at him for a long moment. "Ever wonder why they killed her?"

"What?" Montell raised an eyebrow. "Uh, I don't know. She must have created a scene, tried to stop them from this heinous theft, so they had to silence her violently. She was so brave."

JJ shook her head. "There were no signs of a struggle. The police report says she died of lethal drug poisoning, not a violent attack."

Montell touched his chin. "That's odd."

JJ mocked him by touching her own chin in the same way. "Is it?"

At that, Cooper's doll-like smile twisted into a frown. "What are you insinuating here?"

JJ leaned forward with a steely gaze. "I think you know."

"Winona and I represented the highest end of the casino industry. We are consistently a five-star establishment and the number one employer of choice in Las Vegas. We support local artisans. We give generously to charities."

"Yes, especially that new one, the Nevada Food Bank Charitable Trust."

Montell sighed nervously and sounded exasperated. "Yes, that's one that we support."

"And by support, you mean pay." JJ stood with her arms crossed in front of her chest. "Pay yourself."

"What do you mean, pay myself? It's a legitimate charity." His eyes started to dart around the room.

"Oh, really?"

"Yes, really."

"That's funny, because we did a little digging into donations, bank records. Deep, high-tech digging. What tangled webs we weave..."

"You have a problem with feeding the hungry, Miss Kamaras? With giving to charities?"

"When they're real, no." JJ circled around him like a tiger ready to pounce. "The Nevada Food Bank is a shell company, or in this case, shell charity." JJ gave a disgusted laugh. "It's so Vegas, it's almost a cliché. A front. With proceeds and direct deposits funneled through a bank in the Cayman Islands and straight to one Montell Cooper."

A siren sounded in the distance and Montell's eyes grew wide. "So I started a charity! It's a noble thing. It's what Winona would have wanted!"

"Not exactly. But you planned it well, I must admit," JJ said. "Hiring Frank Gunn and his hit team to kill her. And you nearly got away with it."

"With what?" he asked with a surprised look. "Kill her? She was my colleague!"

JJ looked over his head and smirked. "That was what got me really searching. Why would anyone want her dead? She wasn't a danger to anyone. The more I sat with that question, the closer I came to finding the answer."

"What are you talking about?" His face was becoming increasingly red by the minute.

"She was killed because she got in the way. Your way. Not only to selling the Arapaho but also to selling the countless other pieces of priceless art here at the hotel. As you know, Winona thought art was to be appreciated, not hocked for sale. If there were any proceeds from the unveiling, they'd go to charity. She was the general manager, so she could make that decision. You were only second in charge. You needed her out of the way."

"We were a team!" Montell said in an incredulous tone.

"Well, congratulations on your promotion to general manager," JJ said, dripping in sarcasm. "How very convenient." She glared at him. "You got Gunn's hit team to carry out your requested 'executive services.' What you didn't know is that they got to your own maintenance staff—Rocky, to be exact. I mean, the guy probably makes $10 an hour. Could use an extra ten grand or so for an hour's work, right?

He had the keys to all the rooms. They paid the housekeeper to be a lookout. Rocky goes in and plants the chloroform in Winona's air conditioning unit so she'd be unconscious and not make a ruckus for the big event. That explains the chemical smell and why I felt dizzy when I was in there. But the most clever part of all was Gunn's fake doctor rushing in, acting like he's saving her, when in reality, he was injecting her with pentobarbital. Oh yes, Gunn's team had the angles covered. Then I, without knowing it, made things that much easier for everyone. I was the last to see her alive and became the prime suspect. I even made a call for the doctor myself."

Sirens were audible in the distance and coming closer. Montell started to pant quietly through his snarl.

"What you didn't count on—silly you—was that Gunn and Balvin are as low as they come. You think they'd leave a priceless statue in Winona's room without swiping it for themselves?" She laughed. "You really *are* an amateur."

Montell's jaw tightened.

"*That's* why you needed our help," JJ continued. "What good was your plan without the Arapaho? You thought that with Winona out of the way, you were home free. You'd be in charge and could 'donate' it to your favorite local charity—the Nevada Food Bank Charitable Trust—aka, you—then sell it for all it's worth. But, to your horror, the statue was gone! Oh, how I'd have liked to have seen the look on your face."

"Get out of my office! This is harassment! You were a guest at our esteemed hotel!"

The sirens had grown louder and then stopped outside, leaving an eerie silence.

"You're going to go to prison for a very long time, Mr. Cooper."

"You don't have any proof!" Montell snapped as his eyes darted toward the office door and back again.

"Is that so? The secret records you kept with Simone are being subpoenaed. Might look a tad suspicious when they see a purchase of CHCl3 solution—chloroform—on a purchasing order. And the check for $50 thousand for executive services to Frank Gunn. JJ shook her head mockingly. "Amateur move, my friend. Always pay cash."

Montell swallowed and buried his head in his hands, sounding like he was starting to cry.

"Aw, don't cry and get tears all over your fancy suit. No, there'll be time for that, and with the orange jumpsuit, you won't have to worry about dry cleaning."

Montell exploded out of his chair, raced for the office door, yanked it open, and sprinted past Simone's reception desk into the corridor.

Officer Tyrell and three other officers raced toward him from the opposite direction and surrounded him.

"It wasn't me, officer! I was framed by such bad men! I'm willing to tell you everything they did! I'm the victim here!"

"Save it, Cooper," Officer Tyrell snapped as she grabbed his wrist, twisted it into a hold, and cuffed him. "Read him his rights, Hernandez."

Officer Hernandez stood towering over Montell. "You have the right to remain silent..."

"You have to believe me! I would never kill her. I would never sell the Arapaho!"

"Anything you say can and will be used against you in a court of law..."

"I can't go to prison! Do you know what they'll do to someone like me in there?"

"You have the right to an attorney..."

CHAPTER 28

A new hostess at the museum café ushered JJ inside and led her to where Tony, Logan, Rabbit, Gwen Q, Rebecca, Daniel, and Max were all sitting and waiting.

"Mission accomplished." She pulled out the check she had just collected from Montell. "Looks like we all have a little extra spending money."

"Wrapped up just in time for the big day tomorrow, eh, Logan?" Tony said, slapping him on the back. Sitting in between Logan and Rabbit, he grabbed both of them around the neck and hugged them.

JJ sat between her two best friends and did the same. "We're four for four, detectives." They all smiled and high-fived.

Logan had a quizzical look and turned to Tony. "So, I get why Luke the Stickman was willing to help us—to have Gwen Q for a date, and that Alex wanted to help avenge his aunt Winona's death, but how on earth did you convince Ted Cookie to help?"

"I told you. The guy's ego's the size of Texas. A little flattery goes a long way with him. Told him I needed to see the master in action." Tony laughed, then clapped his hands together. "Okay, so what do we feel like doing our last night in Vegas?"

JJ looked at her old rival, Bond007forlife, then the rest of the group. "I say we play some poker."

"Yes!" Daniel turned toward the others. "Are we in?"

"My last night as a single guy," Logan pleaded to Tony, Rabbit, and Max, all of whom nodded in unison. "We're in."

"Casino time!" Gwen Q called out.

As the group started to disband from the table, Tony approached JJ and pulled her into a tight hug. "You were incredible this week."

"Thanks. You did a great job, too." JJ smiled. "I know it was a little … outside your comfort zone, so thanks for helping."

"No problem." Tony laughed and then hesitated, taking JJ's hand. "So how about, if you're not too busy . . . you know, posing as an art thief or an underboss's girlfriend or leaping between skyscrapers . . . you go with me tonight?"

"I think that sounds amazing." JJ smiled and felt her face grow warm. "Almost like we're . . . dating."

"Ah, dating. As in, beyond casual . . . as in, officially together."

Oh no, I hope I didn't blow it.

Maybe I should take it back.

No, don't be wishy-washy. "Uh, yes. Officially together. As a couple."

He looked at JJ and broke out in a broad smile. "I like the sound of that."

"Me, too." *Yes!* "Great, I'll meet up with you in a bit. I have to make a quick call first, then get dressed—you know, Vegas style."

Tony's eyebrows rose as if picturing Vegas JJ already.

"I'll text you when I'm ready to hit the casino."

"It's a deal," Tony said, walking away with what looked like an undeniable lilt in his step.

The group was gone, and JJ sat alone at the museum café table. She pulled out her phone and tapped the number.

"Julia," the deep, warm voice answered.

"Dad!"

"Everything okay?"

"Yes, fine. You're still up for picking us up at the airport tomorrow, right?"

"But of course."

"Great. And since our flight leaves so early, I'll get there in time to work the brunch with you."

Kostas laughed. "It's okay. You'll probably be tired. Plus, I thought you'd want to get right to your new detective agency work."

"That can wait till Monday. Sunday's for us, Dad." JJ sensed her father's smile. "And also, I wanted to say thanks for your concern about us coming here."

"It was probably unnecessary." He paused. "I just know a few shady characters from the past, from the Jim Thorpe restaurant scene years ago when we were all getting started. They took their pizza place out to Las Vegas and . . . well, it's neither here nor there. But that's why I sent the pepper spray with you. Probably silly."

Pizza place. Tony's uncle and Carmine! "Oh no, actually, I used the pepper spray."

"What!"

"Well, it was sort of a false alarm," JJ clarified. "But I was glad you made me take it."

"Julia . . ."

"Everything's fine, Dad. I'll tell you when I get there. So, is Mom around?"

"Yes, she's folding napkins."

"Can you put her on? I want to tell her something." JJ waited and drummed the table. A smile grew on her face as she heard the familiar clang of pots in the background.

"Julia, my love. Your trip has gone well, I trust?"

"Mom! Yes, it has. Been an … adventure."

"Really? Yes, I suppose Las Vegas can be exciting."

"Yes, for sure. You know, all kinds of . . . crazy stunts going on here," JJ said, recalling the roof-to-balcony leap. "Hey, remember what you taught me about summoning power from my core? Really works."

"Julia, what were you doing?"

"It all worked out. I'll tell you everything tomorrow, Mom." JJ chuckled to herself. *Well, maybe not everything.* "So, what's Jason doing?"

A moment lapsed. "Hey, sis. Descended into a life of drug dealing and prostitution yet?"

"Still as funny as ever." JJ smirked. "No, just here with my girls, staying out of trouble."

"Is Gwen there? Is she asking about me?"

"Yeah, in your dreams."

"Playing hard to get, eh?" He laughed. "Look, I gotta go seat someone. Enjoy Sin City. Here's Dad."

"Hey, Dad, can you leave the hummus for me for tomorrow? I have a new twist on it I'd like to try."

"I'm listening..."

"It's a surprise. Greco-Japanese—that's all I'll say. Except that you were right. Las Vegas isn't like Jim Thorpe or Italy. It's ... well, I just can't wait to see you guys."

When they ended the call, JJ sat at her table in silence and laughed to herself.

It had been quite a week.

Espionage, death-defying leaps, even a casino heist. Well, reverse heist, technically. With one night left and the murder mystery successfully behind her, she trembled with excitement and anticipation at the thought of joining her friends at the casino card tables—and at being the *official* date of the dashing Tony Natale.

Yes, her first trip to Las Vegas had certainly been an experience—an outright, bona fide, movie-worthy adventure.

But part of her was already packed and gone and standing beside her father making dolmades, dazzling him with her new Greco-Japanese fusion hummus. Luckily, she was taking the best of her Vegas trip with her back to good old Jim Thorpe, PA—her beloved friends.

She grinned at the irony of it.

First you can't wait to get somewhere. Then you can't wait to get home.

ALSO BY JOY PATRICK

If you liked this book, #4 in the series,
you'll love the rest!

See what antics JJ and the gang have been up to all along!

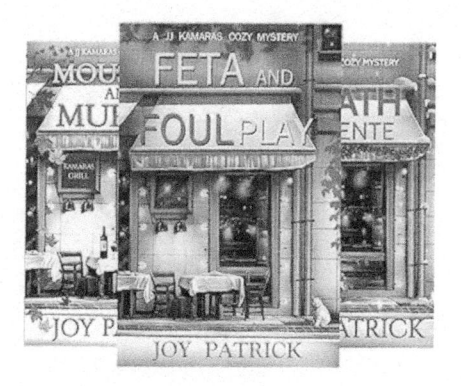

Get my books!

P.S. Book #5 is in the works….. stay tuned!

Made in the USA
Monee, IL
25 April 2024